Flair
FOR MURDER

FRANCES & RICHARD LOCKRIDGE

Introduction by Jeffrey Marks

THE LOST CLASSICS SERIES

Flair
FOR MURDER

FRANCES & RICHARD LOCKRIDGE

Introduction by Jeffrey Marks

Lost Classics

CRIPPEN & LANDRU PUBLISHERS
Cincinnati, Ohio
2024

Cover Design by Jackie Webber

ISBN (limited clothbound edition): 978-1-936363-84-1
ISBN (trade softcover edition): 978-1-936363-83-4

FIRST EDITION

*Printed in the United States of America
on recycled acid-free paper*

Jeffrey A. Marks, Publisher
Douglas G. Greene, Senior Editor

Crippen & Landru Publishers
P. O. Box 532057
Cincinnati, OH 45247
USA

Email: Orders@crippenlandru.com
Web: www.crippenlandru.com

CONTENTS

INTRODUCTION

Couples that Sleuth Together....

A writing couple who created a sleuthing couple, Richard and Frances Lockridge collaborated on Jerry and Pam North for over two decades, publishing twenty-six novels about their adventures. The setting and characters were semi-autobiographical, with the childless writing spouses sharing their home with two Siamese cats.

Richard Lockridge (1898–1982) was born far from New York City, hailing from Missouri. After serving in the First World War, he returned to the Midwest and worked as a journalist at a Kansas City newspaper. In 1922, he married fellow reporter Frances Davis. Ten years later, Lockridge wrote a biography of renowned actor Edwin Booth, the older brother of Abraham Lincoln's assassin, John Wilkes Booth. He was known for his Shakespearean performances, acclaimed as perhaps the best Hamlet ever. The couple moved to New York City after the book's publication.

Mr. and Mrs. North appeared as a bon vivant couple in whimsical short stories in *The New Yorker*. These were collected in 1936 as *Mr. and Mrs. North* and published by the Frederick A. Stokes Company. Lockridge would later claim that their surname came from one of the four bridge positions, more commonly known as the dummy in the game.

After publishing the 1936 book of the Norths, Frances Lockridge suggested a plot for a mystery novel. The couple began to work on the book but struggled with creating the main characters. Eventually, they agreed to use their already familiar characters as the sleuths. Employing a title similar to Richard's first book, they called the mystery *Mr. and Mrs. North Meet Murder*. The authors worked out a future routine, discussing the book's potential plot from Frances's outline, and then Richard wrote the novel. To recognize Frances's participation, the books gave her top billing. Their first work, where the Norths discover a body in the bathtub, is reminiscent of Dorothy L. Sayers's *Whose Body?*

Like the mysteries of Nero Wolfe and Ellery Queen, the stories depicted the life of a married couple in the Big Apple. Jerry works as an editor in a publishing company, and Pam is a homemaker. While Pam can be flighty, she often stumbles across the clues and solves the murder, though not without a scuffle. While the series focuses on the domesticity of the couple, the backgrounds for the crimes include publishing, drama, education, and of course, cats.

The series was immediately popular. The New York couple who owned Siamese cats, frequently named after liquors, charmed readers with their martini-drinking and wit. By January of the following year, Jerry and Pam North, the publisher and sleuthing housewife, were on Broadway, running half a year before closing.

However, the public had not heard the last of the Norths. In 1942, the couple appeared on radio, sharing their escapades with listeners for twelve years. The show won an Edgar for Best Radio Play in 1946 from the newly founded Mystery Writers of America. They shared the award that year with *The Adventures of Ellery Queen.*

Manhattan is a big place, and the Norths' universe expanded quickly. While they were primarily known for working with Lieutenant Bill Weigand, they also collaborated with other police officers. One of these was Lt. Heimrich, whom the crime-solving couple met in their second novel. Indeed, most of the short stories in this collection feature that policeman. Heimrich starred in twenty-two later novels (to the Norths' twenty-six.) In these, the authors' attribution was given as Richard and Frances Lockridge, switching the order from the Norths' series.

They added a third long-running series featuring Nathan Shapiro. That character would cross into a few of the Heimrich novels and appear in ten books.

Starting in 1946, the Norths appeared on television in fits and starts. The show aired on WNBT in New York, reprising the

Broadway play. They appeared in 1949 for twenty-one episodes on *NBC Presents*. In 1952, the show moved to CBS with a new cast, which ran for thirty-nine episodes. The following year, the show aired for eighteen episodes on NBC. Many of the 1950s episodes with Barbara Britton and Richard Denning are still available.

As the 1960s began, the Lockridges were named Grand Masters of the Mystery Writers of America, and two years later, they were given a special award from the organization. In 1963, Frances Lockridge passed away. The Norths' series ended with her death. While Richard would write other series characters, he could not write about the woman modeled after his wife.

Two years later, Richard married Hildegarde Dolson. He wrote a memoir of their courtship, *One Lady, Two Cats*, in which Dolson was a dog-lover while he preferred his Siamese cats. Richard Lockridge died in 1982 after a series of strokes.

The long-running series are still available today and are appreciated by those who enjoy Golden Age mysteries.

Jeffrey Marks
Cincinnati, February 2024

PATTERN FOR MURDER

PATTERN FOR MURDER

Fern Hartley came to New York to die, although that was far from her intention. She came from Centertown, in the Middle West, and died during a dinner party—given in her honor, at a reunion of schoolmates. She died at the bottom of a steep flight of stairs in a house on West Twelfth Street. She was a little woman and she wore a fluffy white dress. She stared at unexpected death through strangely bright blue eyes. . . .

There had been nothing to foreshadow so tragic an ending to the party—nothing, at any rate, on which Pamela North, who was one of the schoolmates, could precisely put a finger. It was true that Pam, as the party progressed, had increasingly felt tenseness in herself; it was also true that, toward the end, Fern Hartley had seemed to behave somewhat oddly. But the tenseness, Pam told herself, was entirely her own fault, and as for Fern's behavior—well, Fern *was* a little odd. Nice, of course, but—trying. Pam had been tried.

She had sat for what seemed like hours with a responsive smile stiffening her lips and with no comparable response stirring in her mind. It was from that, surely, that the tenseness— the uneasiness—arose. Not from anything on which a finger could be put. It's my own fault, Pam North thought. This is a reunion, and I don't reunite. Not with Fern, anyway.

It had been Fern on whom Pam had responsively smiled. Memories of old days, of schooldays, had fluttered from Fern's mind like pressed flowers from the yellowed pages of a treasured book. They had showered about Pam North, who had been Fern's classmate at Southwest High School in Centertown. They had showered also about Hortense Notson and about Phyllis Pitt. Classmates, too, they had been those years ago— they and, for example, a girl with red hair.

"—red hair," Fern Hartley had said, leaning forward, eyes bright with memory. "Across the aisle from you in Miss Burton's English class. Of course you remember, Pam. She went with the boy who stuttered."

I am Pamela North, who used to be Pamela Britton, Pam told herself, behind a fixed smile. I'm not an impostor; I did go to Southwest High. If only I could prove it by remembering something—anything. Any little thing.

"The teacher with green hair?" Pam North said, by way of experiment. "Streaks of, anyway? Because the dye—"

Consternation clouded Fern's bright eyes. "Pam!" she said. "That was another one entirely. Miss Burton was the one who—"

It had been like that from the start of the party—the party of three couples and Miss Fern Hartley, still of Centertown. They were gathered in the long living room of the Stanley Pitts' house—the gracious room which ran the depth of the small, perfect house—an old New York house retaining the charm (if also something of the inconvenience) of the previous century.

As the party started that warm September evening, the charm was uppermost. From open casement windows at the end of the room there was a gentle breeze. In it, from the start, Fern's memories had fluttered.

And none of the memories had been Pam North's memories. Fern has total recall; I have total amnesia, Pam thought, while keeping the receptive smile in place, since one cannot let an old schoolmate down. Did the others try as hard? Pam wondered. Find themselves as inadequate to recapture the dear, dead days?

Both Hortense Notson and Phyllis Pitt had given every evidence of trying, Pam thought, letting her mind wander. Fern was now reliving a perfectly wonderful picnic, of their junior year. Pam was not.

Pam did not let the smile waver; from time to time she nodded her bright head and made appreciative sounds. Nobody had let Fern down; all had taken turns in listening—even the men. Jerry North was slacking now, but he had been valiant. His valor had been special, since he had never even been in Centertown. And Stanley Pitt had done his bit, too; of course, he was the host. Of course, Fern was the Pitts' house guest; what a lovely house to be a guest in, Pam thought, permitting her eyes briefly, to accompany her mind in its wandering.

Stanley—what a distinguished-looking man he is, Pam thought—was with Jerry, near the portable bar. She watched Jerry raise his glass as he listened. Her own glass was empty, and nobody was doing anything about it. An empty glass to go with an empty mind, Pam thought, and watched Fern sip ginger ale. Fern never drank anything stronger. Not that she had anything against drinking. Of course not. But even one drink made her feel all funny.

"Well," Pam had said, when Fern had brought the subject up, earlier on. "Well, that's more or less the idea, I suppose. This side of hilarious, of course."

"You know," Fern said then, "you always did talk funny. Remember when we graduated and you—"

Pam didn't remember. Without looking away from Fern, or letting the smile diminish, Pam nevertheless continued to look around the room. How lovely Phyllis is, Pam thought—really is. Blonde Phyllis Pitt was talking to, Clark Notson, blond also, and sturdy, and looking younger than he almost certainly was.

Clark had married Hortense in Centertown. He was older—Pam remembered that he had been in college when they were in high school. He had married her when she was a skinny, dark girl, who had had to be prouder than anyone else because her parents lived over a store and not, properly, in a house. And look at her now, Pam thought, doing so. Dark still—and slim and quickly confident, and. most beautifully arrayed.

Well, Pam thought, we've all come a long way. (She nodded, very brightly, to another name from the past—a name signifying nothing.) Stanley Pitt and Jerry—neglecting his own wife,

Jerry North was—had found something of fabulous interest to discuss, judging by their behavior. Stanley was making points, while Jerry listened and nodded. Stanley was making points one at a time, with the aid of the thumb and the fingers of his right hand. He touched thumb-tip to successive fingertips, as if to crimp each point in place. And Jerry—how selfish could a man get—ran a hand through his hair, as he did when he was interested.

"Oh," Pam said. "Of course I remember him, Fern."

A little lying is a gracious thing.

What a witness Fern would make, Pam thought. Everything that had happened—beginning, apparently, at the age of two—was brightly clear in her mind, not muddy as in the minds of so many. The kind of witness Bill Weigand, member in good standing of the New York City Police Department, always hoped to find and almost never did—never had, that she could remember, in all the many investigations she and Jerry had shared since they first met Bill years ago.

Fern would be a witness who really remembered. If Fern, Pam thought, knew something about a murder, or where a body was buried, or any of the other important things which so often come up, she would remember it precisely and remember it whole. A good deal of sifting would have to be done, but Bill was good at that.

Idly, her mind still wandering, Pam hoped that Fern did not, in fact, know anything of buried bodies. It could, obviously, be dangerous to have so total a recall and to put no curb on it. She remembered, and this from association with Bill, how often somebody did make that one revealing remark too many. Pam sternly put a curb on her own mind and imagination. What could Fern—pleasant, bubbling Fern, who had not adventured out of Centertown, excepting for occasional trips like these—know of dangerous things?

Pam North, whose lips ached, in whose mind Fern's words rattled looked hard at Jerry, down the room, at the bar. Get me out of this, Pam willed across the space between them. Get me out of this! It had been known to work or had sometimes seemed to work. It did not now. Jerry concentrated on what Stanley Pitt was saying. Jerry ran a hand through his hair.

"Oh, dear," Pam said, breaking into the flow of Fern's words, as gently as she could. "Jerry wants me for something. You know how husbands are."

She stopped abruptly, remembering that Fern didn't, never having had one. She got up—and was saved by Phyllis, who moved in. What a hostess, Pam thought, and moved toward Jerry and the bar. The idea of saying that to poor Fern, Pam thought. This is certainly one of my hopeless evenings. She went toward Jerry.

"I don't," she said when she reached him, "remember anything about anything. Except one teacher with green hair, and that was the wrong woman."

Jerry said it seemed very likely.

"There's something a little ghoulish about all this digging up of the past," Pam said. "Suppose some of it's still alive?" she added.

"Huh?" Jerry said.

He was told not to bother. And that Pam could do with a drink. Jerry poured, for them both, from a pitcher in which ice tinkled.

"Some time," Pam said, "she's going to remember that one thing too many. That's what I mean. You see?"

"No," Jerry said, simply.

"Not everybody," Pam said, a little darkly, "wants everything remembered about everything. Because—"

Stanley Pitt, who had turned away, turned quickly back. He informed Pam that she had something there.

"I heard her telling Hortense—" Stanley Pitt said, and stopped abruptly, since Hortense, slim and graceful (and *so* beautifully arrayed) was coming toward them.

"How Fern doesn't change," Hortense said. "Pam, do you remember the boy next door?"

"I don't seem to remember anything," Pam said. "Not anything at all."

"You don't remember," Hortense said. "I don't remember.
Phyllis doesn't. And with it all, she's so—sweet." She paused.
"Or is she?" she said. "Some of the things she brings up—
always doing ohs, the boy next door was. How does one do an
oh?"

"Oh," Jerry said, politely demonstrating, and then, "Was he
the one with green hair?" The others looked blank at that, and
Pam said it was just one of the things she'd got mixed up, and
now Jerry was mixing it worse. And, Pam said, did Hortense
ever feel she hadn't really gone to Southwest High School at all
and was merely pretending she had? Was an impostor?

"Far as I can tell," Hortense said, "I never lived in Centertown.
Just in a small, one-room vacuum. Woman without a past."
She paused. "Except," she said, in another tone, "Fern remem-
bers me in great detail."

Stanley Pitt had been looking over their heads—looking at
his wife, now the one listening to Fern. In a moment of silence,
Fern's voice fluted. "Really, a dreadful thing to happen," Fern
said. There was no context.

"Perhaps," Stanley said, turning back to them, "it's better to
have no past than to live in one. Better all around and safer."

He seemed about to continue, but then Clark Notson joined
them. Clark did not, Pam thought, look like a man who was
having a particularly good time. "Supposed to get Miss Hartley
her ginger ale," he said. He spoke rather hurriedly.

Jerry, who was nearest the bar, said, "Here," and reached
for the innocent bottle—a bottle, Pam thought, which looked a
little smug and virtuous among the other bottles. Jerry used a
silver opener, snapped off the bottle cap. The cap bounced off,
tinkled against, a bottle.

"Don't know your own strength," Clark said, and took the
bottle and, with it, a glass into which Jerry dropped ice. "Never

drinks anything stronger, the lady doesn't," Clark said, and bore away the bottle.

"And doesn't need to," Hortense Notson said, and drifted away. She could drift immaculately.

"She buys dresses," Pam said. "Wouldn't you know?"

"As distinct—?" Jerry said, and was told he knew perfectly well what Pam meant.

"Buys them for, not from," Pam said.

To this, Jerry simply said, "Oh."

It was then a little after eight, and there was a restless circulation in the long room. Pam was with Phyllis Pitt. Phyllis assured her that food would arrive soon. And hadn't old times come flooding back?

"Mm," Pam said. Pam was then with Clark Notson and, with him, talked unexpectedly of tooth paste. One never knows what will come up at a party. It appeared that Clark's firm made tooth paste. Stanley Pitt joined them. He said Clark had quite an operation there. Pam left them and drifted, dutifully, back to Fern, who sipped ginger ale. Fern's eyes were very bright. They seemed almost to glitter.

(But that's absurd, Pam thought. People's don't, only cats'.)

"It's so exciting," Fern said, and looked around the room, presumably at "it." "To meet you all again, and your nice husbands and—" She paused. "Only," she said, "I keep wondering . . ."

Pam waited. She said, "What, Fern?"

"Oh," Fern said. "Nothing dear. Nothing really. Do you remember—"

Pam did not. She listened for a time, and was relieved by Hortense, and drifted on again. For a minute or two, then, Pam North was alone and stood looking up and down the softly lighted room. Beyond the windows, at the far end, lights glowed up from the garden below. The room was filled, but not harshly, with conversation—there seemed, somehow, to be more than the seven of them in it. Probably, Pam thought, memories crowded it—the red-haired girl, the stuttering boy.

Fern laughed. Her laughter was rather high in pitch. It had a little "hee" at the end. That little "hee," Pam thought idly, would identify Fern—be something to remember her by. As Jerry's habit of running his hand through his hair would identify him if, about all else, she suddenly lost her memory. (As I've evidently begun to do, Pam North thought.) Little tricks. And Fern puts her right index finger gently to the tip of her nose, presumably when she's thinking. Why, Pam thought, she did that as a girl, and was surprised to remember.

Her host stood in front of her, wondering what he could get her. She had, Pam told him, everything.

"Including your memories?" Stanley Pitt asked her. Pam noticed a small scar on his chin. But it wasn't, of course, the same thing as—as running a hand through your hair. But everybody has something, which is one way of telling them apart.

"I seem," Pam said, "a little short of memories."

"By comparison with Miss Hartley," Stanley said, "who isn't? A pipe line to the past. Can't I get you a drink?"

He could not. Pam had had enough. So, she thought, had all of them. Not that anybody was in the least tight. But still . . .

Over the other voices, that of Fern Hartley was raised. There was excitement in it. So it isn't alcohol, Pam thought, since Fern hadn't had any. It's just getting keyed up at a party. She looked toward Fern, who was talking, very rapidly, to Jerry. No doubt, Pam thought, about what I was like in high school. Not that there's anything he shouldn't know. But still. . .

Fern was now very animated. If, Pam thought, I asked whether anyone here was one cocktail up I'd—why, I'd say Fern. Fern, of all people. Or else, Pam thought, she has some exciting surprise.

It was now eight-thirty. A maid appeared at the door, waited to be noticed, and nodded to Phyllis Pitt, who said, at once, "Dinner, everybody." The dining room was downstairs, on a level with the garden. "These old stairs," Phyllis said. "Everybody be careful."

The stairs were, indeed, very steep, and the treads very narrow. But there were handrails and a carpet. The stairway ended in the dining room, where candles glowed softly on the table, among flowers.

"If you'll sit—" Phyllis said, starting with Pam North. "And you and—" They moved to the places indicated; "And Fern—" Phyllis said, and stopped. "Why," she said, "where is—"

She did not finish, because Fern Hartley stood at the top of the steep staircase. She was a slight figure in a white dress. She seemed to be staring fixedly down at them, her eyes strangely bright. Her face was flushed and she made odd, uncertain movements with her little hands.

"I'm—" Fern said, and spoke harshly, loudly, and so that the word was almost a shapeless sound. "I'm—"

And then Fern Hartley, taking both hands from the rails, pitched headfirst down the staircase. In a great moment of silence, her body made a strange, soft thudding on the stairs. She did not cry out.

At the bottom of the red-carpeted stairs she lay quite still. Her head was at a hideous angle to her body—an impossible angle to her body. That was how she died.

Fern Hartley died of a broken neck. There was no doubt. Six people had seen her fall. Now she lay at the bottom of the stairs and no one would ever forget her soft quick falling down that steep flight. An ambulance surgeon confirmed the cause of her death and another doctor from up the street—called when it seemed the ambulance would never get there—confirmed it, too.

But after he had knelt for some time by the body the second doctor beckoned the ambulance surgeon and they went out into the hallway. Then the ambulance surgeon beckoned one of the policemen who had arrived with the ambulance, and

the policeman went into the hall with them. After a few minutes, the policeman returned and asked, politely enough, that
they all wait upstairs. There were, he said meaninglessly, a few
formalities.

They waited upstairs, in the living room. They waited for
more than two hours, puzzled and in growing uneasiness.
Then a thinnish man of medium height, about whom there was
nothing special in appearance, came into the room and looked
around at them.

"Why, Bill!" Pam North said.

The thinnish man looked at her, and then at Jerry North, and
said, "Oh." Then he said there were one or two points.

And then Pam said, "Oh," on a note strangely flat.

How one introduces a police officer, who happens to be an
old and close friend, to other friends who happen to be murder
suspects—else why was Bill Weigand there?—had long been
a moot question with Pam and Jerry North. Pam said, "This
is Bill Weigand, everybody. Captain Weigand. He's—he's a
policeman. So there must be—" And stopped.

"All right, Pam," Bill Weigand said. Then, "You all saw her
fall. Tell me about it." He looked around at them, back at Pam
North. It was she who told him.

Her eyes had been "staring"? Her face flushed? Her movements uncertain? Her voice hoarse? "Yes," Pam said, confirm-
ing each statement. Bill Weigand looked from one to another of
the six in the room. He received nods of confirmation. One of
the men—tall, dark-haired but with gray coming, a little older
than the others—seemed about to speak. Bill waited. The man
shook his head. Bill got them identified then. The tall man was
Stanley Pitt. This was his house.

"But," Bill said, "she hadn't been drinking. The medical examiner is quite certain of that." He seemed to wait for
comment.

"She said she never did," Pam told him.

"So—" Bill said.

Then Hortense Notson spoke, in a tense voice. "You act," she said, "as if you think one of us pushed her."

Weigand looked at her carefully. He said, "No. That didn't happen, Mrs. Notson. How could it have happened? You were all in the dining room, looking up at her. How could any of you have pushed her?"

"Then," Clark Notson said, and spoke quickly, with unexpected violence. "Then why all this? She . . . what? Had a heart attack?"

"Possibly," Bill said. "But the doctors—"

Again he was interrupted.

"I've heard of you," Notson said, and leaned forward in his chair. "Aren't you Homicide?"

"Right," Bill, said. He looked around again, slowly. "As Mr. Notson said, I'm Homicide." And he waited.

Phyllis Pitt—the pretty, the very pretty, light-haired woman—had been crying. More than the rest, in expression, in movements, she showed the shock of what had happened. "Those dreadful stairs," she said, as if to herself. "Those dreadful stairs."

Her husband got up and went to her and leaned over her. He touched her bright hair and said, very softly, "All right, Phyl. All right."

"Bill," Pam said. "Fern fell, downstairs and—and died. What more is there?"

"You all agree," Bill said, "that she was flushed and excited and uncertain—as if she had been drinking. But she hadn't been drinking. And . . . the pupils of her eyes were dilated. That was why she seemed to be staring. Because, you see, she couldn't see where she was going. So . . ." He paused. "She walked off into the air. I have to find out why. So what I want. . ."

It took him a long time to get what he wanted, which was all they could remember, one memory reinforcing another, of what had happened from the start of the dinner party until it ended with Fern Hartley, at the foot of the staircase, all her memories dead. Pam, listening, contributing what she could, could not see that a pattern formed—a pattern of murder.

Fern had seemed entirely normal—at least, until near the end. They agreed on that. She had always remembered much about the past and talked of it. Meeting old school friends, after long separation, she had seemed to remember everything—far more than any of the others.

"Most of it, to be honest, wasn't very interesting." That was Hortense Notson. Hortense looked at Pam, at Phyllis Pitt.

"She was so sweet," Phyllis said, in a broken voice.

"So—so interested herself," Pam said. "A good deal of it was pretty long ago, Bill."

Fern had shared her memories chiefly with the other women. But she had talked of the past, also, with the men.

"It didn't mean much to me," Stanley Pitt said. "It seemed to be all about Centertown, and I've never been in Centertown. Phyllis and I met in New York." He paused. "What's the point of this?" he said.

"I don't know," Bill Weigand told him. "Not yet. Everything she remembered seemed to be trivial? Nothing stands out? To any of you?"

"She remembered I had a black eye the first time she saw me," Clark Notson said. "Hortense and I—when we were going together—ran into her at a party. It was a long time ago. And I had a black eye, she said. I don't remember anything about it. I don't even remember the party, actually. Yes, I'd call it pretty trivial."

"My God," Stanley Pitt said. "*Is* there some point to this ?"

"I don't know," Bill said again, and was patient. "Had you known Miss Hartley before, Mr. Pitt?"

"Met her for the first time yesterday," Stanley told him. "We had her to dinner and she stayed the night. Today I took her to lunch, because Phyl had things to do about the party. And—" He stopped. He shrugged and shook his head, seemingly at the futility of everything.

"I suppose," Jerry North said, "the point is—did she remember something that somebody—one of us—wanted forgotten?"

"Yes," Bill said. "It may be that."

Then it was in the open. And, with it in the open, the six looked at one another; and there was a kind of wariness in the manner of their looking. Although what on earth I've got to be wary about I don't know, Pam thought. Or Jerry, she added in her mind. She couldn't have told Jerry anything about me. Well, not anything important. At least not very . . .

"I don't understand," Phyllis said, and spoke dully. "I just don't understand at all. Fern just—just fell down those awful stairs."

It became like a game of tennis, with too many players, played in the dark. "Try to remember," Bill had told them; and it seemed they tried. But all they remembered was apparently trivial.

"There was something about a boy next door," Phyllis Pitt remembered, "A good deal older than she was—than we all were. Next door to Fern. A boy named—" She moved her hands helplessly. "I've forgotten. A name I'd never heard before. Something—she said something dreadful—happened to him. I suppose he died of something."

"No," Hortense Notson said. "She told me about him. He didn't die. He went to jail. He was always saying 'oh.' " She considered. "I think," she said, "he was named Russell something." She paused again. "Never in my life, did I hear so much about people I'd never heard of. Gossip about the past."

Stanley Pitt stood up. His impatience was evident.

"Look," he said. "This is my house, Captain. These people are my guests. Is any of this badgering getting you anywhere? And . . . where is there to get? Maybe she had a heart attack. Maybe she ate something that—" He stopped, rather abruptly; rather as if he had stumbled over something.

Weigand waited, but Pitt did not continue. Then Bill said they had thought of that. The symptoms—they had all noticed the symptoms—including the dilation of the pupils, might have been due to acute food poisoning. But she had eaten almost nothing during the cocktail period. The maid who had passed canapés was sure of that. Certainly she had eaten nothing the rest had not. And she had drunk only ginger ale, from a freshly opened bottle.

"Which," Bill said, "apparently you opened, Jerry."

Jerry North ran his right hand through his hair. He looked at Bill blankly.

"Of course you did," Pam said. "So vigorously the bottle cap flew off. Don't you—"

"Oh," Jerry said. Everybody looked at him. "Is that supposed—"

But he was interrupted by Pitt, still leaning forward in his chair. "Wait," Pitt said, and put right thumb and index finger together, firmly, as if to hold a thought pinched between them. They waited.

"This place I took her to lunch," Stanley said. "It's a little place—little downstairs place, but wonderful food. I've eaten there off and on for years. But . . . I don't suppose it's too damned sanitary. Not like your labs are, Clark. And the weather's been hot. And—" He seemed to remember something else and held this new memory between thumb and finger. "Miss Hartley ate most of a bowl of ripe olives. Said she never seemed to get enough of them. And . . . isn't there something that can get into ripe olives? That can poison people?" He put the heel of one hand to his forehead. "God," he said. "Do you suppose it was that?"

"You mean food poisoning?" Weigand said. "Yes—years ago people got it from ripe olives. But not recently, that I've heard of. New methods and—"

"The olives are imported," Pitt said. "From Italy, I think. Yes. Dilated pupils—"

"Right," Bill said. "And the other symptoms match quite well. You may—"

But now he was interrupted by a uniformed policeman, who brought him a slip of paper. Bill Weigand looked at it and put it in his pocket and said, "Right," and the policeman went out again.

"Mr. Notson," Bill said, "you're production manager of the Winslow Pharmaceutical Company, aren't you?"

Notson looked blank. He said, "Sure."

"Which makes all kinds of drug products?"

Notson continued to look blank. He nodded his head,

"And Mr. Pitt," Bill Weigand said. "You're—"

He's gone off on a tangent, Pam North thought, half listening. What difference can it make that Mr. Notson makes drugs— or that Mr. Pitt tells people how to run offices and plants bet- ter—is an "efficiency engineer"? Because: just a few minutes ago, somebody said something really important. Because it was wrong. Because—Oh! Pam thought. It's on the tip of my mind. If people would only be quiet, so I could think. If Bill only wouldn't go off on these—

"All kinds of drugs," Bill was saying, from his tangent, in the distance. "Including preparations containing atropine?"

She heard Clark Notson say, "Yes. Sure."

"Because," Bill said, and now Pam heard him clearly—very clearly— "Miss Hartley had been given atropine. It might have been enough to have killed her, if she had not had quick and proper treatment. She'd had enough to bring on dizziness and double vision. So that, on the verge of losing consciousness, she fell downstairs and broke her neck. Well?"

He looked around.

"The ginger ale," Jerry said. "The ginger ale I opened. That . . . opened so easily. Was that it?"

"Probably," Bill said. "The cap taken off carefully. Put back on carefully. After enough atropine sulphate had been put in. Enough to stop her remembering." Again he looked around at them; and Pam looked, too, and could see nothing—except shock—in any face. There seemed to be fear in none.

"The doctors suspected atropine from the start," Bill said, speaking slowly, "But the symptoms of atropine poisoning are very similar to those of food poisoning—or ptomaine. If she had lived to be treated, almost any physician would have diagnosed food poisoning—particularly after Mr. Pitt remembered the olives—and treated for that. Not for atropine. Since the treatments are different, she probably would not have lived." He paused. "Well," he said, "what did she remember? So that there was death for remembrance?"

Phyllis Pitt covered her eyes with both hands and shook her head slowly, dully. Hortense Notson looked at Weigand with narrowed eyes and her husband with—Pam thought—something like defiance. Stanley Pitt looked at the floor and seemed deep in thought, to be planning each thought between thumb and finger, when Weigand turned from them and said, "Yes?" to a man in civilian clothes. He went to talk briefly with the man. He returned. He said the telephone was a useful thing; he said the Centertown police were efficient.

"The boy next door," Weigand said, "was named Russell Clarkson. He was some years—fifteen, about—older than Fern Hartley. Not a boy any more, when she was in high school, but still the boy next door. He did go to jail, as you said, Mrs. Notson. He helped set up a robbery of the place he worked in. A payroll messenger was killed. Clarkson got twenty years to life. And—he escaped in two years, and was never caught. And—*he was a chemist*, Mr. Notson. As you are. Mr. *Clark* Notson."

Notson was on his feet. His face was very red and he no longer looked younger than he was. He said, "You're crazy! I can prove—" His voice rose until he was shouting across the few feet between himself and Weigand.

And then it came to Pam—came with a kind of violent clarity. "Wait, Bill. *Wait!*" Pam shouted. "It wasn't 'ohs' at all. Not *saying* them. That's what was wrong."

They were listening. Bill was listening.

Then Pam pointed at Hortense. "You," she said, "the first time you said *doing* ohs. Not saying 'Oh.' You even asked how one *did* an oh. We thought it was the—the o-h kind of O. But—it was the *letter* O. And—*look at him now!* He's doing them now. *With his fingers.*"

And now she pointed at Stanley Pitt, who was forming the letter O with the thumb and index finger of his right hand; who now, violently, closed into fists his betraying hands. A shudder ran through his body. But he spoke quietly, without looking up from the floor.

"She hadn't quite remembered," he said, as if talking of something which had happened a long time ago. "Not quite." And he put the thumb and index finger tip to tip again, to measure the smallness of a margin. "But—she would have. She remembered everything. I've changed a lot and she was a little girl, but . . ."

He looked at his hands. "I've always done that, I guess," he said. He spread his fingers and looked at his hands. "Once it came up," he said, "there would be fingerprints. So—I had to try." He looked up, then, at his wife. "You see, Phyl, that I had to try?"

Phyllis covered her face with her hands.

After a moment Stanley Pitt looked again at his hands, spreading them in front of him. Slowly he began to bring together the fingertips and thumb tips of both hands; and he studied the movements of his fingers intently, as if they were new to him. He sat so, his hands moving in patterns they had never been able to forget, until Weigand told him it was time to go.

Nobody Can Ask That

NOBODY CAN ASK THAT

It had been the easiest case in Captain Heimrich's very considerable experience. Five hours ago—five hours and a few minutes, at the most—a man had been beaten to death where a driveway joined a narrow blacktop road in the Town of Van Brunt, County of Putnam, State of New York.

The man who had killed sat across a desk from Captain Heimrich and did not deny his guilt. The man's thin and sensitive face was tormented, and his eyes were blank, but he did not deny he had killed Robert Ashton, a man in his middle thirties who had spent the previous afternoon on a golf course.

The previous afternoon had been surprisingly warm for mid-spring. Now, at a little before one on a.m. Monday morning, it was still surprisingly warm—"unseasonably warm," the Weather Bureau called it. A window in the Town House, which Heimrich had borrowed, was partially open, and the air which came through it was almost like summer air. This uncharacteristically pleasant weather was one of several things which Malcolm Burns, retired cartoonist, had not counted on. For one reason and another, Captain Heimrich of the New York State Police was rather sorry for Malcolm Burns although Heimrich knows of no excuse for murder.

"I admit killing him," Burns said, and his voice was steady—painfully steady. "What more do you want?"

A statement was wanted. A statement was always wanted. It would be taken down, transcribed, and Mr. Burns would be asked to sign it. The third man in the room was a police stenographer. Mr. Burns was aware of that.

"I killed him," Burns said. "I beat him over the head with this." He touched the heavy cane which rested against the chair he sat in. "I said, 'Walked down to meet you, old man,' and he said something—I don't remember what—and started up the drive ahead of me. I hit him hard. Then I hit him a couple more times to make sure. That's a statement. I'll sign that, Captain."

Momentarily, Captain Heimrich closed the bright blue eyes set wide in a square face. He said, somewhat sadly, "Now, Mr. Burns," and added that they needed more than that. Then he said, "Because you thought he was in love with your wife?"

"Does Lydia know yet?" Malcolm Burns asked. "Has somebody told her?"

"Yes," Heimrich said "Somebody's running her up from town."

Burns nodded, to show he had heard. Then he said, "I'd known he was in love with her for quite some time. She's—she's easy to fall in love with. But ..." He stopped. His face worked. "She was beginning to fall in love with him," he said. "She didn't know it herself but—I could hear it in her voice. When she spoke of him."

"Only that?" Heimrich said.

"I know Lyddie," Burns said. "Don't you think I know her? Her voice—she can't hide things in her voice. She's not that kind. And ..." Again he stopped. Heimrich waited. "She's the straightest thing in the world," Burns said, and spoke very slowly, in a very steady voice. "When—when she realized she loved him, she'd come to me and tell me. And—she'd go away. Get a divorce and ..." Once more he stopped.

"She was all I had left," he said, and spoke as if everything were dead around him. "What more?"

"From the beginning," Heimrich said. "Start with Saturday. You'd arranged for your wife to go to New York to see her mother. You agreed to call Ashton and tell him the usual Sunday evening supper was off. You didn't call him. You gave your housekeeper Sunday off."

"She's always off Sunday," Burns said. "Most of them are, around here. She made a casserole to go into the oven for Sunday supper. I'd been out walking—walking up and down the drive—and came up to the house just as she was leaving. She told me where the casserole was and that everything was finished up and that she'd remembered to wind the clock and set it."

"She told you that she had set the clock?"

"It runs slow," Burns said. "Every Saturday she winds it and sets it. Every Saturday she tells us she has."

"Go on," Heimrich said. "On Sunday? Before you went down the drive to meet Mr. Ashton?"

Burns did not see what difference it made now. But—if Heimrich did—he had waited until it was time. He had had breakfast. He had simply sat there and played some records. And—he had been lonely. Was that a satisfaction to Heimrich? He had been lonely. But, all he had done was to wait until it was time. Everything else had been done.

Heimrich said he had "arranged" for his wife to go to New York. That was not true; was not, at any rate, simply true. She had had her mother on her mind; had said often that she ought—really ought—to go and spend a day with her. "I encouraged her," Burns said. "That was all. Suggested she go some Saturday afternoon, stay until Monday. She picked last Saturday. But one weekend would have been as good as another. He came every Sunday, or almost. Had for, oh, about a year."

The even voice faltered, momentarily. Heimrich waited.

Malcolm Burns had fixed himself lunch. Then he had gone out onto the terrace and sat in the sun—faced the afternoon sun. From the terrace one could ... He interrupted himself. "You've seen it."

Heimrich had seen it. He had driven up the narrow, turning driveway, bordered close by tall evergreens. He had come out into the clearing where the Burns house hugged its hilltop. He had seen the terrace, which was to the west of the house. From the terrace, one could look far across the Hudson; could look along a wide vista cut through trees; could see the river far below and the hills—tinted now with spring—beyond. The sun had just set behind the Palisades when Heimrich went to the house, and the sky flamed there.

"We cut the trees," Burns said, as if Heimrich had spoken. "Mostly by ourselves, Lyddie and I. So that we could sit on the terrace and look across the river. That was one reason we built there. So that . . ."

He stopped. He said Heimrich couldn't, he supposed, be less interested. He said he had sat on the terrace, in the sun. It was nobody's business what he had thought about. After a time he had gone back in and changed into dark clothes. After that, he had made himself a drink. "One drink," he said. "I was getting a little jumpy." He had turned the record player on again, at low volume, and listened to music and—waited. He found that time passed very slowly. "You'd think it wouldn't," he said. "But it did."

The clock struck, and he counted its striking. It struck six, and he went back to his chair and waited, listening to the soft music. He found that the music, instead of soothing, became a torment. "We listened to music a good deal, Lyddie and I," he said. "Especially the last couple of years." He turned the player off and merely sat, waiting. The clock struck the half hour, and then he got up and went around the house turning on lights.

"People can see the house from the road," Burns said. "At a certain point. I didn't want him to see it dark and think the plans were changed."

He put the casserole in the oven, then. He got his cane and sat in a chair near the door. The time passed so slowly that he had a sudden conviction the clock had stopped, and made himself listen intently and heard the clock ticking. "It's amazing what you can hear if you try," he said. "Too much, sometimes. A note in a voice and . . ." He did not finish. He said, across the desk to Heimrich, "What use is this to you?"

"Go on," Heimrich said. "We like to get things clear."

Finally, Burns went on, the clock struck seven. He waited until it struck the half hour, and then a few minutes more. Ashton was due at a quarter of eight. He did not want to have to wait "down there" too long. But he wanted to be in good time.

"You didn't think of the Knights?" Heimrich asked him.

"Sure, I thought of them," Burns said. "I'm not a fool, Captain. I had the whole thing worked out. They'd be inside, with the lights on. You look out of a lighted room into the dark, and what do you see? Not a thing. Not even through that big window of theirs."

"That's true, naturally," Heimrich said, and remembered the wide "picture" window of John Knight's house—and the house itself not far back from the blacktop road, opposite the entrance of the Burns driveway. He remembered the terrace which ran along the front of the Knight house, and the terrace furniture the Knights had got out early this season, because it had turned so unusually warm. "You thought it would be blamed on these hoodlums who've been going around?"

"Why not?" Burns said. "It wouldn't be the first time young gangsters have killed a man. But I told you—I didn't care who you pinned it on. Or tried to pin it on. That was the beauty of it. It was so damned simple. Where would you have started? What would you have had to go on?"

"All right," Heimrich said. "Go ahead."

Burns had walked down the driveway, which was like a tunnel, walled and topped by trees. At the foot of the driveway he had had to wait only a few minutes, and then he heard Ashton's familiar steps on the road surface. "He always," Burns said, "walked as if he owned the earth." He greeted Ashton, and was greeted in return. Ashton started up the drive, and Burns brought the heavy cane up and down again.

He felt the shock of the impact through the cane and then, in the same instant, the—it was a kind of "give"—as Ashton's skull was broken. He stooped over Ashton, lying on the graveled drive, and made sure. But to make more than sure he struck again—struck twice, flailing downward with the cane. Then he walked back up the drive to his house and, when he was there, washed the cane off under a tap in the kitchen and dried it with tissue and flushed the paper down a toilet.

"You didn't hear anything?" Heimrich asked him.

"A man shouting," Burns said. "Oh—I know. But Knight is always yelling at that dog of his."

He waited a few minutes more, and then telephoned to Ashton's house and asked the housekeeper whether Ashton was on his way—said Ashton was late, and that it wasn't like him to be late. He was told that Ashton had left some time before.

He had planned that, after waiting a little, he would walk down the driveway and find the body. But—

"Ten or fifteen minutes and you came," Burns said to Heimrich, and his face worked and it was, evidently, an effort to keep his voice steady. "You must have been close by."

"At the Old Stone Inn," Heimrich said. "They got me there a few minutes after Mr. Knight called and said what he had seen—what they'd all seen—from the terrace."

"I had quite an audience," Malcolm Burns said, and now he made no effort to keep bitterness—the bitterness of defeat— out of his voice. "The Knights and their guests. Any other—"

"Yes," Heimrich said. "Any other day than the last Sunday in April, Mr. Burns. The day we start daylight saving hereabouts. So that, when the clock struck seven, it was only six by what people call sun time. And the sun was well up—didn't set for almost an hour. It was still bright day when you killed him at a quarter of eight." He paused and looked at the twisting features of the man across from him, and at the still, blank eyes. "Your housekeeper," Captain Heimrich said, "told you she had set the clock."

"I explained about—" Burns began, and then spread his hands hopelessly. His face, with that gesture, seemed somehow to fall apart. He began groping for his cane, like an old, blind man. But he was not old. He was not over forty.

"She was my eyes," he said, and spoke in a low, dazed voice. "If she went away . . ." He did not, he could not, immediately, finish. His groping fingers found the heavy cane. "You can't ask a man to lose his eyes twice," Burns said. "Nobody can ask that."

THE SEARCHING CATS

THE SEARCHING CATS

The cat appeared soundlessly on the open window sill—the window which had been forced open. The cat was spotlessly black and for a moment, poised there, he looked around the room with unblinking yellow eyes.

The cat looked at M. L. Heimrich, Captain, New York State Police, a man most often concerned with homicide, and now so concerned. The cat looked away again, dismissing the man. The cat dropped to the polished tile floor of the living room. Then he spoke, once, on a note which seemed to Heimrich to have a curious insistence. The cat seemed to wait for an answer.

When there was no answer, the cat began to move—to glide around the floor, nose close to the floor. The cat's progress was erratic; the cat circled among chairs and under tables; now and then the cat paused and Heimrich could see his nostrils quiver. But always he went on again, engrossed and, it seemed to the watching man, impelled Heimrich had never before seen a cat behave so—search so. Search, Heimrich decided after a time for something he would never find again.

"It's no good, fellow," Heimrich said, and the cat paused and looked up, as if he had understood the words and waited to be told more. (Which was, of course, absurd.) "Your man's dead, fellow," Heimrich said, and the cat still seemed to wait. "Murdered," Heimrich told him. The cat waited a moment longer and then went back to sniffing the green tile floor.

Heimrich, having other things to do, walked across the living room, ignored by the black cat, and out of the small, pleasant, country house. It was about four o'clock, then, in the afternoon.

At a few minutes after four, Russell Ashby circled his white farmhouse and sounded the horn of the pickup truck to tell Jane he was home. He ran the truck into the shed which served as a garage and walked back to the house—a tall man in slacks and a jacket with suede-patched elbows. He took long strides on the path to the house and, when he saw Jane standing in the doorway, began to nod his head and smile at her.

It was a kind of pantomime of triumph. But the set expression—was it of anxiety?—on his wife's young face did not alter, and then Ashby slapped his left hip pocket, where his wallet was, to make what should have been evident, clearer yet. But still her face did not brighten.

He walked up on the porch, his footsteps emphatic on the boards. She stepped out onto the porch to meet him and there was an odd rigidity in her slender body, matching the rigidity of her face—a rigidity unbecoming to so lovely a face.

"Got it," Russell Ashby said. "All I had to do was ..." He stopped; her eyes stopped his words. "What's the matter, baby?" he said, in a very different tone.

"Russ," she said, "where have you been?"

"Been?" he said. "What's the matter, Jane? You knew—" He broke off. "Oh," he said, "afterward. That's it. Think I'd got run over? Went to look at Jenkins's north field. See if it's worth haying. Took longer than—"

"Russ," Jane Ashby said, and her young voice shook. "Russ—Mr. Bailey's dead. They say—Russ, they say somebody killed him. Broke into the house and—killed him. Russ—somebody from the police called. Wanted—"

She did not go on. He held her close and could feel her body trembling. Over her head he looked, flatly, at nothing. And waited. After a time, stumbling on the words, she told him what everybody around East Belford had known for an hour or more. "Everybody but me," Russell Ashby said, his voice steady, uninfected.

Thwaite Bailey, the richest man around, had been found dead by his daughter, who had walked the hill path from the "big" house to her father's house at about three o'clock. She had telephoned him first and got no answer, and had been worried and walked the quarter of a mile which separated the original Bailey house from the low, contemporary house Bailey had built for week ends when he turned the old house—too big for anybody, the old house was—over to his daughter and Sidney Combe, her husband.

Margaret Combe had found her father dead in the doorway of his bedroom, his head crushed. She had found the little house, which had so much glass it glittered like a jewel in its green valley, ransacked.

"They think he was taking a nap," Jane Ashby said, sitting straight in her living room. "That somebody broke in, thinking he wouldn't be there in the middle of the week. And that whoever it was made a noise that wakened Mr. Bailey and then—killed him. Russ . . ."

"Yes?" Russell Ashby said.

"Russ—Sid says Mr. Bailey had a lot of money in the house. A—a thousand dollars. That he always had. And—it isn't there, Russ. *It isn't there!*"

"No," Russ Ashby said. "It's in my pocket."

She put hands over her eyes—the biggest ever, he thought. The brownest ever.

"Hold it, baby," Russ said. "Like we planned—I said, did he want to invest in an outfit that needed a push over a hump. Because of the way he and Dad felt about each other. I made a pitch, Jane. And—look." He took his billfold from his hip pocket and they both looked—looked at twenty fifty dollar bills. "I said a check would be just as good but he said, 'Here son. Take it.' It was—a gesture, I guess. He was always a little like that."

Thwaite Bailey had been like that, as a good many people knew. It was a quirk. Rich men—and men as generous in service as with money—are entitled to quirks.

"Russ," she said, "when were you there?"

"About two," he said.

"He'd been dead about an hour," Jane Ashby said, "when Marge found him. They say that . . . Russ, did anybody see you? I mean? Because . . ."

He looked at her strangely. "You mean," he said, "because of that other thing?"

She did not answer. That was good enough, or bad enough. "It was a long time ago," Russ Ashby said, slowly.

It had been—long before Clint Ashby had died and left his son, a dairy farm which was now—in spite of everybody's advice—an Aberdeen Angus breeding farm; long before Russ went to Korea in the Marines. It had been before Russ Ashby grew up; when he was a "wild kid." With other wild kids he had broken into a closed country house. "For the hell of it."

But Russell Ashby had been the one caught—and booked. Clinton Ashby had made good and the charges had been dropped. But . . .

"Sid was walking his dog," Russell Ashby, the grown-up Russell Ashby, said now. He spoke slowly. "On the hill. He was going away when I saw him—his back was to me. Swinging that squire's walking stick of his. I left the truck on Shady Lane and cut across by the path . . ."

Someone knocked at the front door. The knocking was not loud. There was no threat in it.

"Russ," Jane said, in a very low voice, a hurried voice. "Russ—I'm scared. *Terribly scared.* They won't believe . . ."

Russell Ashby went to the door and let in two large, solid men—men not in uniform; Captain M.L. Heimrich and Sergeant Charles Forniss, of the New York State Police.

Heimrich said, "Mr. Ashby?" and then, "We'd like to ask you a couple of questions." Heimrich and Forniss did not wait for more, but went on into the living room. "Oh," Heimrich said. "Mrs. Ashby?" She was a remarkably pretty young woman, he thought; she looked frightened. Which was reasonable. She nodded her head, standing, fear in her face. "Sit down," Heimrich said, and then, "You, too, Mr. Ashby." He waited until they sat down. Then he sat on a straight chair. Forniss remained near the door, standing, looking very large.

"Mr. Thwaite Bailey was killed this afternoon," Heimrich said. "About the time you were there, Mr. Ashby."

Heimrich closed bright blue eyes. And waited. And Jane Ashby, fear rioting in her eyes, waited, too.

Waiting, she held her breath. That was evident to Heimrich—the cessation, utter if momentary, of breath movement in her body. Heimrich looked at Russell Ashby and Ashby looked only at his wife—and looked as if he listened. Heimrich saw Ashby's chest rise, slowly. It seemed a long time before Russell Ashby spoke.

"I was there," Ashby said. "He was all right when I went in—when he let me in. He was all right when I left."

"Yes," Heimrich said, "you were there. Your fingerprints are there. On the desk drawer."

"Maybe," Ashby said. "I don't know what I touched. I've said I was there. Mr. Bailey was an old friend of Father's. Of mine, too. I dropped by to see him now and then. He—"

"Your prints are on record," Heimrich said. "From the other time. You know what I mean?"

Again Russell Ashby and his wife looked at each other—looked quickly, then away again. Ashby said, "I know what you mean."

"The same thing," Heimrich said. "Except—murder, this time. A window forced. But this time—a man killed."

"I was a kid then," Ashby said. "A long time ago, when I was a kid."

"Yes," Heimrich said. "Mr. Combe—Sidney Combe—says you were carrying something when you left the house. He couldn't make out what it was. He was taking a walk—walking his dog. It was about two o'clock, he says. You went out of the house and around it toward the path that leads down to Shady Lane. Walking very fast, Mr. Combe says."

"Most of the time," Russ Ashby said, "I walk fast. Most of the time I take the path. I wasn't carrying anything. Sid's wrong about that."

"Better show him, Charlie," Heimrich said, and Forniss went out the door. He came back almost at once. He carried a stick of firewood—a stick about three feet long and a little over two inches in diameter; a stick like a club. "Found it halfway down the path," Heimrich said. "To where you parked your car in the lane. And—there's blood on this, Mr. Ashby. Not a lot. Didn't bleed much, Mr. Bailey didn't. But—enough."

"I don't know anything about it," Ashby said. "You claim this was what I was carrying? You claim it's got my prints on it?

"Now, Mr. Ashby," Heimrich said. "Rough wood. Wouldn't take prints worth anything, naturally. It was used to force the window. The way you and the other kids forced the other window. Then—to kill Mr. Bailey." Heimrich paused.

"Mr. Combe says his father-in-law had about a thousand dollars in the desk drawer. Says he kept it there as—as a kind of petty cash. Mr. Combe's term for it."

He watched. For a moment neither of the Ashbys spoke. Then—slowly, as if so simple a movement were incredibly difficult—Jane Ashby brought her hands from her eyes. Heimrich could see no expression in her eyes.

"He loaned it to us," she said, in a voice which was blank like her eyes. "Show them, Russ."

Russell Ashby looked at her for a long moment. Then he showed them. Heimrich took the crisp bills out of Ashby's billfold, riffled them, put them back, then put the billfold in his own pocket.

"We'll give you a receipt for this, Mr. Ashby," Heimrich said. "At the station house."

They left Jane Ashby then—left her sitting in a chair, with her face buried in her hands again, her slender body shaking again. "I'll be back," Russell Ashby said, and she did not seem to hear him.

That was about five o'clock. At a quarter after seven, Heimrich went into the taproom of the Maples Inn, on the main street of East Belford, and ordered a before-dinner drink. He sipped the drink and thought of murder—and of the tall young man at the police station, still denying murder. A stubborn young fool, Russell Ashby was, to deny what was so obvious.

Heimrich sighed. He thought of Ashby's dark-haired wife— was she sitting so, with hands hiding her face, shutting out a world which had crumbled? There was no good in thinking of that.

He thought, instead, of Margaret Combe, who had gone through a bright afternoon to invite her father over for tea. If it was necessary to think of such things, think of her white face, *her* blank eyes. With nobody better, stronger, than Sidney Combe to stand with her.

Combe, the country squire—Ashby had called him that, bitterly, but, Heimrich thought, with reason. Tweeds and walking stick and dog on rawhide leash—and with the seven forty-three to catch five mornings a week to a job in town which wasn't much more than a clerk's job. Well Combe wouldn't have to go back from his two-week vacation. He could spend the rest of his life walking his dog. He—

Heimrich, who had been looking at nothing, found he was looking at another cat. This cat was yellow. Another tom, from the shape of the forelegs—a big yellow cat standing in the doorway of the taproom and looking at Heimrich, and looking away again. I don't, Heimrich thought, seem to interest cats. The cat came into the taproom and began to sniff the floor. Two cats in one day, sniffing intricate patterns around a floor. Yellow cat and black cat, both searching. Yellow cat and—

"Marty," Heimrich said, through the service window of the bar, "what's he doing that for?"

The bartender looked at the cat.

"Smells something," Marty said. "Mrs. Latham's peke, most likely. Brought it in with her, while back. If he bothers you—"

"Not me," Heimrich said, and watched the cat's systematic sniffing of the floor, watched the yellow cat follow the scent where the little dog had gone. "Does he smell around after people?" Heimrich asked, and Marty shook his head. He said that cats don't care much how people smell. Only other cats, and dogs—

"You don't want dinner?" Marty said, because Heimrich stood up abruptly.

"Not now," Heimrich said, and went to his car, and drove toward the old Bailey house a few miles out of East Belford—toward the house, and a white-faced woman and a rather strutting man, who wouldn't have to catch the seven forty-three any more, now that his wife had inherited a few million dollars; toward a man who would be free, now, to walk his boxer on a leash any day he chose—and to take him along on leash when he went to call on people. Toward a man, at any rate, who had planned on that freedom, and might have got it but for a cat who followed a dog's scent around a room. A persistent cat, following a scent.

"I've come to have a look at that walking stick of yours," Heimrich told Sidney Combe, at the door of the old house—told a tweedy Sidney Combe, with his boxer sitting behind him, attentive, in the hall. Combe merely looked at Heimrich. "To see if there are blood traces on it," Heimrich said. "Hard to get blood off things, the lab boys tell me—"

Combe was a fool—but a frightened man maybe—to try to slam the door on Heimrich. Heimrich had a foot in it.

"Now, Mr. Combe," Heimrich said. "That's no good. Where would you go? Your mind was working better earlier. When you smeared a little of Mr. Bailey's blood on the club, for example. And planted it on the path. When you took advantage of the fact that Ashby went around for a loan, and you saw him.

When you tried to make it all look like a robbery, because Ashby broke into a place when he was a kid. Disappointed not to find the money, Mr. Combe? Mr. Bailey had given it to Ashby. But that worked out all right, too, or looked like working—"

Combe gave up trying to close the door. He said he didn't know what Heimrich was talking about.

"Now, Mr. Combe," Heimrich said. "A black cat, among other things. Cats can't testify, naturally. But I watched the cat and—I can at testify, you know."

Combe really didn't know what Heimrich was talking about, then Heimrich told him, later, about the cat—told him after he had got the East Belford substation on the telephone and said to let Russell Ashby go and come pick Sidney Combe up. Heimrich followed the police car which had Combe in it only as far as the Maples Inn. He stopped off there to finish his dinner. He started into the tap room but stopped at the door.

Russell and Jane Ashby were sitting at a corner table, with food in front of them, and no great interest in food. They were looking at each other as if, to the other, each was new. They wouldn't want to see him, Heimrich thought. They had each other to look at—and a whole future to talk about.

A future, Heimrich thought that a past might have ruined, but fortunately had not. Thanks, in large part, to a dead man's cat—inquisitive, as cats are notoriously. And, Heimrich thought, as policemen have need to be, however obvious the truth seems.

DEAD BOYS DON'T REMEMBER

DEAD BOYS DON'T REMEMBER

The bus stopped at the head of Blueberry Lane and red warning lights blinked fore and aft. Behind it, two cars halted obediently, and then a third came round the bend of the state road and stopped, too. One car, with equal obedience, pulled up facing the blue-and-yellow school bus, and that was at 3:20 of a Friday afternoon in late May.

Rodney Burke got off the bus, carrying his schoolbooks. He was towheaded and sturdy and a few months more than ten years old. The boys and girls who remained in the bus made shrill sounds, as if something very exciting were happening.

There was nothing actually exciting under way—School Bus No. 3, of District No. 1, had made its scheduled stop at Blueberry Lane, so that Rodney Burke could get off and walk half a mile along a shaded, little-used road to the sprawling white house he lived in. It was the back way home; the conventional way was by the town road which paralleled the state road, and it was on the town road that the Franklin Burke house fronted—fronted distantly, as became so large a house, so deep in spreading lawns.

Several of the boys and girls yelled, "'Bye, Rod!" as if he were going on a long journey from which return was improbable. Rod waved and yelled back—yelled, "Bye, kids," as if this were indeed a parting. Then, bareheaded, the sun bright on his bright hair, he walked into the lane—walked out of the sun into the shade, into the flecked pattern of shadow and sunlight which moved gently on the road surface.

The road curved after a hundred yards or so and Rodney Burke—walking in the middle of the roadway, wearing a striped shirt and denim trousers and sneakers—went around the bend in the lane, out of sight from the state road. But the bus had pulled away by then.

It takes a boy of ten varying times to walk half a mile on a shady lane, depending on how much of a hurry he is in and, of course, on what shows up. If deer show up, for example, he stops to look at deer, partly because deer look so expectantly at people, partly because they are very pretty creatures, and when they finally decide to bound away the white of their tails is like froth on breaking waves.

But Rod was seldom a boy to dawdle: he was a boy of projects, most of which involved building something. Usually he came up the garage drive—sometimes running—within ten minutes after the bus stopped, and one could set clocks by the bus.

Janice Burke was working in her annual garden, partly because it needed weeding—as didn't it always?—and partly because it was an experience of infinite sweetness to see her son coming along the drive, with the afternoon sun bright on his hair. Janice was a little flushed—it was quite warm for May— and she was a little older than most mothers of boys of ten.

The Burkes had waited a dozen years before they had had a child, so that Rodney had seemed rather a miracle. He still did. They tried, of course, not to let him know it, nor make too much of an only child. "We mustn't fuss over him," they told each other, and usually managed not to.

Is it "fussing" over a boy to notice if he takes ten minutes longer than usual to walk half a mile through a lane in which there are no perils? There is no reason to be anxious if he is twenty minutes later than usual—probably the bus is late. But at twenty minutes of four, Janice Burke stood up in her garden and shielded her blue eyes with a grubby hand as she looked into the sun, since the boy would come out of the sun. And five minutes later she walked—to meet him, she told herself— along the garage drive and around the garage, where the field road ran down to Blueberry Lane. When she saw the field road empty, she began to hurry and then to call, "Rod, Rod?"

When she ran back from the empty lane, her breath came shudderingly. In the house she went to the telephone and drew deep, but still shuddering, breaths as she dialed, and tried to make her voice steady as she spoke. But her voice still shook. Rod had left on the bus with the others; they were sure of that at the school. And the bus had been on time, and Rod had got off at the usual place. Harry Bigham, who drove the school bus and had just returned to the garage from his last trip, was sure of that.

Janice Burke was reaching toward the telephone again, but it rang under her hand and she snatched at it. She said, "Yes?" in a voice not like her own.

"Mrs. Burke?" a man's voice said, and she said, "Yes. Oh, *yes!*"

"We've got the boy," the man said. It was a voice like any voice. "We'll tell you what to do tomorrow. You hear what I'm saying?"

"Yes," she said. *"Yes! Rod is—"*

"He'll be all right if you do what we tell you," the man said. "If you pay what we tell you." And then his voice faded, as he turned from the telephone. But she could hear him say, "Bring the kid here."

Then she heard Rod's voice—oh, his voice, *his* voice. "Mama?" Rod said. *"Mama!* They—"

She heard a click and the telephone was dead. She called into it—called the boy's name. Then she fainted. Franklin Burke, coming home early from the city, walked into the living room in time to see his wife sway in the chair and fall from it.

Janice came quickly back to an ugly world and clung to her husband, shaking—and told him.

It was not a decision which many have to make; it is a decision to be reached in agony. Nothing one does is better than any other thing, surer than any other. Franklin Burke called the State Police, to whom country people turn most readily. The police told him, when they came—not noisily and as much as possible by back roads—that he had done the right thing, and hoped they were telling him the truth.

They told him, too, that it looked like the work of professionals, and that the chances were better if that was so. Professionals wanted money; they wouldn't panic; wouldn't—they didn't finish that, or need to, and again they hoped that they were right.

"I'll pay anything," Franklin Burke said, "anything I've got . . ."

"Only," the captain in charge of Troop K said at Hawthorne Barracks, "only, the kid's ten, isn't he? Old enough to remember faces. Remember places. He won't remember if he's dead."

"No," Captain Heimrich—Captain M. L. Heimrich, whose concern is with murder—said. "No, he won't remember if he's dead. He may be already."

They did not, of course, say that to the Burkes—to the tall, gray-haired man with face set hard, to the white-faced woman, whose eyes stared in terror and disbelief, and who would not let a doctor give her sedatives. "I've got to be here," she said, and said it over and over and over, "be here when he comes back." But the Burkes knew without being told . . .

The polish of professional crime showed in several ways. On that the various police agencies agreed—and by Saturday morning everybody was in on it. The police of the villages and cities of Westchester and Putnam counties were in on it, and the sheriffs of the counties, and the New York City Police and the F.B.I. And, of course, the New York State Police, with whom it began. They all agreed the crime was professional, and probably the work of city professionals, since professionals are, for the most part, city men.

There was the deftness of the kidnapping itself. It was not by chance that a car had waited at just the right time, just the right distance along the lane, for Rodney Burke. (The car had pulled to the soft shoulder of the narrow lane and left tire tracks.) It was not by chance that the boy was the son, and the only son, of people with the money the Burkes had, or that their house, and the lane leading toward it, were isolated in the town of Van Brunt, near the Hudson.

It was not by chance that the letter which came in Saturday's mail was typed (new typewriter, almost without idiosyncrasies) on white paper one could buy anywhere, or that there were no fingerprints to guide, except those of postal clerks on the envelope. The letter had been mailed in midtown Manhattan. The letter read:

Price is $100,000. Raise it by Monday and you will be told what to do. It will be tough for the boy if you get new bills, or big ones.

All planned, the police thought—shrewdly planned, with no amateurs involved. Ruthlessly planned. They'll kill him, Captain Heimrich thought, one man in thousands hunting a stolen child—hunting with nothing much to go on, and nothing much to hope for, and haunted by the memory of a woman whose eyes looked and looked, and saw nothing. Probably dead already, Heimrich thought, on Saturday afternoon, as he followed a lead which would take him nowhere.

They had, after some thought, decided to let the newspapers have it. Professionals would know already that the police were in it; the outermost filaments of the web they lived in would have quivered that news to the center.

If enough people heard about it, somebody might see something, remember something. Many did, of course. Leads came from everywhere. Rodney Burke, age ten, fair hair, blue eyes, eighty-four pounds, was everywhere.

By Saturday afternoon he had been seen as far away as the West Coast. (The police doubted that. A car had been used, probably still was being used. But they checked everything, since anything was possible.)

A boy (surely Rod) had been seen running along a sidewalk in Mt. Kisco. They found the boy, who had been going to the grocery for his mother, and running because he wanted to run. (And who did not look at all like Rod.) The Virginia State Police closed in on a motel in Emporia because a boy was crying loudly in one of the rooms and sobbing out, "I want to go home." The boy was six. He was crying because he wanted to go home.

Heimrich, alone in an unmarked car—the police were spread thin to spread wide—drove down a long, rough driveway toward a house secluded in the woods. He drove down the drive because somebody had seen a car drive down it earlier, and somebody was quite sure the people who owned the house were in Europe. They were going on as little as that.

The house, when Heimrich came to it, was a rather large house—a house which had accumulated largeness over years. It was set in a green cup of lawn, with woods edging it. There was a car, with city license plates, parked where the drive widened. Heimrich stopped close behind the city car and got out, and as he got out a man came to the door of the house, and then onto the flagstones.

He was a young man in a polo shirt and slacks—a pleasant-looking young man, who smiled at Heimrich pleasantly. Heimrich told him about Rodney Burke and the smile vanished and the man swore. He said that kidnapping was the dirtiest business there was.

"Yes," Heimrich said. "This is your house, Mr.—?"

"Baxter," the man said. "No. Friends letting me use it. Only been here a couple of hours. Drove up from town and—" He stopped. His eyes narrowed. "Empty house," he said. "You think—?"

"Now, Mr. Baxter," Heimrich said. "We're looking everywhere, naturally. You've been through the house?"

"All this?" Baxter said, and motioned toward the sprawling house behind him. "Must be a dozen rooms. All we need is a couple of them." He paused. "Got friends coming up later," he said, and then, "You want to look? Come on."

He might as well, as long as he was there, Heimrich said. But it would be time wasted, as the morning had been time wasted, and now half the afternoon.

It was. They went together from room to room—looked into the attic and the basement, looked in bedrooms and kitchen and in three shining bathrooms. "Nice place," Baxter said, as they came into the living room, with the house searched and nothing found. "Lucky people. How about a drink?"

"No," Heimrich said. "I'll be getting on. Thanks for—" He stopped, as if listening. Baxter waited.

"Wish I could do more," Baxter said.

"Yes," Heimrich said, but not as if he were answering the pleasant young man in slacks and polo shirt. It was, instead, as if Baxter's voice had interrupted something, as if music were playing which Heimrich strained to hear.

"You hear water dripping anywhere?" Heimrich said. "Bathrooms? Kitchen?"

Baxter looked surprised, puzzled. Then he shook his head slowly, and listened, too. Listening carefully, he heard a faint sound which seemed to come from everywhere, and from nowhere—a kind of grating sound, rhythmical, with metallic pings marking the beat. The sound had just begun.

"I hear it now," Baxter said. "Just barely hear it. Something running in the house? Refrigerator, or—"

"Probably," Heimrich said. "Well, sorry to have bothered you, Mr. Baxter."

It might work that way. Heimrich went out onto the terrace, with Baxter in the living room, looking after him curiously. Heimrich looked around for what he wanted and found it. It was near the edge of the grass, a cube of cement blocks rising three feet above the lawn. It was capped by a heavy metal cover.

Heimrich started to walk toward it, and Baxter came out of the house and watched him. A pocket of Baxter's slacks bulged, heavily. So it wasn't going to be that way.

Heimrich whirled as Baxter reached toward the heavy pocket, and Heimrich was the quicker. "Now, Mr. Baxter," Heimrich said in his soft voice from behind a steady revolver, "we'll go have a look in the pump house. Good place to lock a small boy up in, wouldn't it be? Cover too heavy for a boy to lift and—*better drop it, Mr. Baxter.*"

The man who called himself Baxter dropped it. He wasn't pleasant-looking any more. He went ahead of Heimrich toward the concrete cube.

"Get the cover off," Heimrich told Baxter, and Baxter got the cover off. It was heavy enough—far too heavy to be moved by a boy who, to push against it, would have to balance himself on iron rungs set close to the inner wall of the pump house.

The boy balanced himself on the rungs now and started to come out—and saw Baxter and started to go down again.

"All right, son," Heimrich said. "All right, Rod. You can come out, now."

It was like hide-and-go-seek, and the game over, and everybody home safe. Rodney Burke came out, blue eyes wide. He shrank away a little from Baxter, who did not move, and looked at Heimrich and said, "Are you a policeman, sir?"

"Yes," Heimrich said. "How did you start up the pump?"

"Anybody knows that," Rodney told him, and was evidently surprised that everybody did not. "There's a faucet. So they can drain the tank to clean it. And when the water comes out, the pressure goes down and the pump starts and—"

"Of course," Heimrich said, gravely, and kept his revolver pointed at Baxter, who had never heard of this before.

"It's an old-style pump," Rod said. "Metal pipes. They use plastic now, mostly. Because with metal pipes the noise the pump makes telegrams—no, *telegraphs* through them and into the house—"

"Yes," Heimrich said. "See it now, Mr. Baxter? Water pumps don't start up until enough water's been run out of the pressure tank. And—*there wasn't any water running in the house, was there?*"

"I saw a car come up," Rodney said. "Through the little window. The venti—ventilator? And I thought I'd just try. Maybe somebody'd hear. Because when I yelled nobody could—"

He stopped. "Gee," he said. "I left the water running. Pump the well dry."

Before Heimrich could do anything, Rodney seemed to bounce to the top of the pump house. He went down into it. He came back out of it. "All right now," Rodney Burke, country boy, trained to country ways, said, and the sun was bright on his bright hair.

Baxter, city man, used to city ways, looked at Rodney Burke. He began to shake his head slowly. It had looked like a perfect setup—a perfect place to keep a boy in until he decided what to do with him. How was a city man to know?

ALL MEN MAKE MISTAKES

ALL MEN MAKE MISTAKES

All Men Make Mistakes—But may hope, as is so often optimistically said, to profit by them. Captain M. L. Heimrich, of the New York State Police, considered that he had made his share, and without deriving any profit—mistakes in his trade commonly lead to increased obscurity in situations already sufficiently murky. Today's mistake—the mistake he had made an hour or so earlier on a pleasant afternoon in mid-July—was therefore unique It had proved illuminating.

Surprisingly illuminating Heimrich thought, as he steered his recently purchased car off NY-11F onto a narrow black-topped road in the Town of Van Horn, County of Putnam The car purred uphill—Heimrich turned into an even narrower road and continued to climb until the Hudson River lay far below and the road, twisting, clung precariously to the hillside. Off this road, three days before, James Latham had plunged his heavy convertible off the road and into a deep ravine, where the car landed with wheels in air and Latham under it. Under it and, as was to be expected, dead. The wheels of the car had spun for a time—then spun ever more slowly, as if the car itself were slowly dying.

Arthur Madison, powerless to do more, had watched the spinning wheels and, when Police Corporal Ray Crowley arrived, on summons, had told Crowley about it—dully, but as if the fact were important, which of course—it was not. The shocked mind clings to small certainties, as Crowley, although a young man, had already discovered. And Arthur Madison, who had been waiting, white-faced, when the police car arrived, was obviously in a condition of shock.

"He drove right off," Madison told Crowley, after the policeman had found there was nothing to be done for Latham. "As
if he hadn't even tried to make the turn." They walked farther
up the hill, to Madison's house at the very top. (Blood had run
out from under the car, and there was no point in standing and
looking at it.) They had walked up a steep, curving driveway.
"I stood right here," Madison said, holding out a hand and
pointing down the drive. The hand shook. "It was an awful
thing to—" He did not finish.

"These things happen," Crowley said, and looked down the
drive to where, at right angles, it met the narrow town road. Just
before it reached the road, the drive pitched down abruptly. (It
would be a mean pull in slippery weather, Crowley thought.)
He listened to Madison and could see it happen—see the big
convertible, with the top open, go down the steepness of the
drive toward the hairpin turn to the road.

"He wasn't going very fast," Madison said. "He slowed
for the turn, so it couldn't have been the brakes. The car had
started into the turn, which was to the left. And then—"

"He quit turning and just drove off," Madison said. "The
car—I guess it must have hit a stump or something-it twisted
over almost in a somersault and—" Madison raised both shaking hands and put them over his eyes, as if the sight of the
pitching car was still fixed in his eyes. "I ran down," Madison
said. "I thought he might have been thrown clear. But—you
saw it.

"Jim said to me, 'It looks good. Be seeing you,'" Arthur
Madison told Crowley. "He got in the car and started down
the drive and—" (The shocked mind marks time by repetition.)

"Yes," Crowley said. "What did he mean, 'It looks good,'
Mr. Madison?" That was something to say, something to steady
Madison's shaken mind. Madison did not appear to hear him.
The question was not worth repeating, but then Madison said,
"Oh. A gadget. I invent gadgets. Jim—Jim Latham puts up

money for things like that. He'd come to look at this one. I got it out of the shop and showed him, how it worked and—"

"Sure," Crowley said. "I see. Had he been drinking?"

He had not, Madison said, and the medical examiner, after an autopsy the next day, said the same. The autopsy was a routine matter. It was all a routine matter, at the start. It is one of the tasks of the state police to determine the causes of accident. Latham had been, when the car crashed down on him, a sober man, and apparently in excellent health. There had been nothing wrong with his heart. If, starting the turn he had never finished, Latham had suddenly lost consciousness, there was nothing to explain why.

The police turned to the car itself, which was battered but had sustained little structural damage. It would roll again—it was a new car and still rugged—less than one thousand miles showed on the speedometer of course, they mean an odometer — a common error and not worth correcting. And there was nothing to indicate that in those last few seconds it had in any way failed the man who drove it to his death. Nothing was wrong with the steering mechanism, and nothing indicated that the brakes had failed.

The information was duly passed along to Corporal Crowley, at the Van Horn substation of Troop K.

If one is to be a good policeman, which was Ray Crowley's biggest aim in life, one must believe that there is no effect without a cause. A sound car, driven at reasonable speed on a dry road by a sound man, does not willfully plunge into a ravine. That conviction became a burr in Ray Crowley's mind.

An explanation was obvious—James Latham had chosen this method to kill himself. Crowley knew something of Latham by that time. He decided to find out more. When his relief came on that Tuesday evening, with Latham twenty-four hours dead, Crowley changed to civilian clothes and went to talk to people who had known the dead man—unmarried, as it turned out, thirty-eight, reasonably prosperous, living in Peekskill, and, as

Madison had said, a man who invested money in things from which he expected to get more money.

"What they call a promoter," Crowley explained the next morning, sitting beside a desk that Captain Heimrich was using in the Hawthorne barracks. Crowley had gone through channels to get to Heimrich, as he had done once or twice before when he had come on something that formed a burr in his mind. "And from what I gather, this man Madison hated his guts. Maybe with reason. Latham sounds like he must have been a smart operator."

"You mean that Madison thought he had been cheated?" Heimrich asked. "Gone into a deal with Latham and perhaps been frozen out? Is that the story going around?"

Crowley said, "Yes."

Heimrich, who preferred people to say "Yes" if that is what they mean, closed his bright blue eyes briefly. Then he said, "Go ahead, Ray."

"Madison was broke, the story is," Crowley said. "Because he was broke, his wife left him. You'd think a woman who'd do that would be good riddance, but—"

"Now, Ray," Heimrich said, "that may have been only what Madison told himself, naturally. Because he didn't want to dig deeper. All the more reason to be bitter at Latham, perhaps. Find someone else to blame."

"I don't know," Crowley said.

"No," Heimrich said. "Neither do I. Hate him enough to kill him, you think? You've talked to people. I haven't. To get him up there to look at a new invention, tell him bygones, and then arrange for him to die?"

"The accident's fishy," Crowley insisted. "Latham doesn't seem to be a man who'd kill himself—at least, there's no reason I heard of. People who knew him say the idea's crazy." Crowley paused. "What it comes to, I guess," he said, "is that I've got a hunch—nothing but a hunch"

"There's nothing wrong with a bunch," Heimrich told him. "A policeman is no good who doesn't have hunches. But—how, Ray? He didn't feed Latham poison and they didn't find anything wrong with the car."

"Mr. Madison's an inventor," Crowley said. He said it with no special confidence. "Maybe—Only, he goes in for household gadgets, can openers. Things like that."

"No death rays?" Heimrich said. "No devices to guide a car by remote control?"

Crowley blushed. He was still young enough to blush.

"I know," Heimrich said. "But we need something like that, don't we? Something we can put up to Mr. Madison and get him to explain. You haven't been back to talk to him?"

"No," Crowley said. "What's there to ask him about?"

"Nothing," Heimrich said. "Don't go to him, Ray. But mosey around a little more. Listen to some more things. I'll fix it with your sergeant. I think maybe you're a good man with a hunch, Corporal."

Ray Crowley went to "mosey." Heimrich returned to another investigation—one which had simmered down to a need for proof, and for that only. To prove what one knows is often a tedious business; fortunately, it is almost always possible.

Heimrich was still in search of proof in this other matter, at about three o'clock Thursday afternoon. He was in Peekskill looking for a place to park, and it was then he made his mistake. It was, he thought at the time, a very foolish mistake. Half a block ahead he saw a car begin to pull out from the curb and since there was a car a little behind him which also seemed to have parking on its mind, Heimrich hurried. He turned into the vacant space, to establish his claim, with further maneuvering to come. He went in rather rapidly, and put his brakes on.

And ran right up on the curb.

In fact, he ran over the curb and even a little way onto the sidewalk before he could bring his car to a stop. It was as if the car, so exceptionally docile during the two months he had driven it, had sought to wrench itself from his hands. And had momentarily succeeded.

Heimrich slid the gear selector to reverse and was conscious that people on the sidewalk—although he had not, fortunately, endangered anyone—looked at him with resentment and, he supposed, contempt. A man shook his head pityingly. Heimrich found that his motor was dead, which did nothing to lessen his embarrassment. He started the motor, backed off the sidewalk, parked—and now the car was its responsive self again. Then he started to go about his business.

But he did not.

Instead, he sat for some seconds regarding the dashboard. He told himself he'd be damned, then pulled out and drove to a service station. The head mechanic listened and said, "Sure."

"Sure," he said. "What did you think Captain? Power steering works off the motor. If the motor stalls you're back in conventional steering. But you're not set for that, see, not after you've got used to the easy way. Makes even this baby"—he patted Heimrich's car with affection—"handle like a truck. Happened to a man I know and before he could adjust to it he was—"

"But why," Heimrich said, "should my motor stall? The car was moving and it's a new car too."

"Most likely," the mechanic said, opening the hood and looking inside, "just needs an adjustment. See?" Take your foot off the accelerator and this rod"—he pointed—"bounces back and cuts off the gas. But not all the way off,' cause then you stall. This little rubber gimmick, see, is supposed to stop it in time. What's happened here is"—he took out pliers—"just needs to be reset." He used the pliers, pulled the accelerator rod, and the motor roared. He released the rod and the motor purred. "That's all there is to it, Captain," and he closed the hood.

"A man," Heimrich said, "could tinker with that so a car would stall?"

"Sure," said the mechanic. "But what would anybody want to do that for?"

"And you say a car with power steering and the motor dead would handle like a truck? On a curve, say, when you weren't set for it?"

"Just like I told you, Captain. This man I know had it happen. Ran into a tree and—"

Heimrich thanked him and found a telephone; he asked that Corporal Ray Crowley be found, and instructed. Then he drove north in his recently purchased car with power steering—with power steering of the same type that had been in the heavy convertible under which James Latham had died. Heimrich drove on NY-11F until he came to a narrow, black-topped road which climbed steeply toward the lonely house of Arthur Madison, gadget inventor. Crowley would meet him there, which was only fair to the young corporal with the hunch.

"What would anybody want to do that for?" The automobile mechanic had asked. Heimrich had not answered. But the answer was he thought, very obvious—and very ugly. It would, naturally, be difficult to prove, if Madison stuck to his guns. Fortunately for policemen, amateur murderers seldom do once one knows exactly what questions to ask. A knotted lie unravels easily when one knows which strand to tug at. . . .

HIT-AND-RUN

HIT-AND-RUN

It was Walter Brinkley's first contact with the New York State Police, as it had also been his first contact with violent death. He found the police courteous and patient: telling them what had happened somehow lessened the impact of the violence, so that the quivering of his nerves lessened. It was true that they continued to call him "Professor," an appellation which, although accurate enough, he preferred to hear used in a classroom, which this certainly was not.

"The fog had lifted, then?" the uniformed sergeant said, and the other policeman held his pencil ready. "You appreciate it might make a good deal of difference."

Mr. Brinkley nodded his head. His thick white hair glinted in the sunlight which, at that hour of an April morning, poured into his living room.

"Just," he said. "Very suddenly. Ten minutes before I went down I could hardly see the road. Then I could see the mail box, and that Mr. Beale had been by and put down the flag." He paused. "I call it the flag," he said, a little anxiously. "The arm, you know? The—indicator? That shows when there is mail to be picked up?" He was anxious to be clear. At the same time, he felt he was too anxious. A fussy old man, they would think him. In short, a professor. No wonder . . .

"Yes, Professor," the sergeant said. "And you went down and found Mr. Gray?"

He had. It was all clear in his mind—too clear. He had walked down his driveway, which ran straight up from Hayride Lane for three hundred feet, to his comfortable white house. He had walked in the warming sun of an April morning, and had walked with spring in his steps. He had taken the mail out of his box and looked up and down the road, as one does. And there, not a hundred yards away to the north, just by the big lilac clump at the corner of the Farmers' land, a man lay in the shallow roadside drainage ditch. Walter Brinkley ran, then.

The man was Martin Gray, who lived up the lane half a mile or so, who walked down the lane a mile each decent morning and walked back up the mile, for his health's sake, and who was dying when Brinkley knelt beside him, though he still managed to speak. Now the sergeant wanted to get his last words down very carefully, and Walter Brinkley repeated them as carefully as he could.

"He said," Brinkley told the policeman, "*'Wrong side. Wrong side.'* He spoke more loudly than—than one would have expected. Then he said, *'No! No!'* I suppose as—as a kind of protest?"

"Probably," the sergeant said. "When he saw the car coming at him. Then?"

"Then—*'No!'* again and then, *'No con—'* And then—then he died." It was all clear—dreadfully clear. "I was trying to lift him up," Walter Brinkley, professor emeritus of English, said in a fixed voice, and looked at the sergeant through fixed eyes.

"Nothing you could have done," the sergeant promised him.

And the trooper who was taking notes said, "C-o-n? That was what it sounded like?"

"Well," Brinkley said, and knew he was being fussy again. "Yes. Or k-u-n, perhaps. As if . . ." He felt that they were being very patient with a white-haired, elderly man—an absurdly meticulous man. "That was what it sounded like," he said, firmly, and then, by the way of showing he was not unaware of idiom and knew a little about the world, "A hit-and-run case?"

"Looks like it," the sergeant said. "Didn't see him in the fog. Thought he was dead or—didn't care, long as he could get away. Probably no other car in sight. Well—thanks, Professor. Nothing you could have done you didn't do. Probably want your evidence when we catch up with him."

They seemed very sure they would catch up with the motorist who had killed Martin Gray, Professor Brinkley thought, watching the police car go down the drive. Poor Gray, who had come to North Wellwood only two years ago, retired in his late fifties with, obviously, plenty of money; a strong and active man, considerate of his health. A man with a much younger wife and a pretty daughter by an earlier marriage. Professor Brinkley, a widower and sometimes lonely, returned to his study and work on *American Regional Accents* (tentative title). It was best to return, as quickly as one might, to life's routine.

The police routine had already begun. When a car hits a man hard enough to crush him, the car is damaged. Right front fender, most probably, in this case—car moving south in Hayride Lane, meeting a man, walking north. The man walked to face traffic (if he knew his way around) and stepped out into the roadway because he had to get past a big lilac clump growing too close to the road's edge. Considering the fog, an accident. Until the driver left the scene, and a man dying. A crime, then.

Since Brewster, New York, is north of North Wellwood, the discovery of a light car in a Brewster garage, undergoing repairs on a dented left front fender, seemed without significance. It seemed that until routine disclosed that the car was registered in the name of Constance Gray, and that Constance Gray was Mrs. Martin Gray. Then the matter seemed one for Captain M. L. Heimrich, New York State Police, whose concern is homicide.

Constance Gray was not at home; she was in New York, and neither the maid nor the pretty, sobbing girl—Mary Gray, a senior at North Wellwood High School, called from class to be told of her father's death—knew where Constance could be reached. She was expected back in the late afternoon, expected on the train due in Brewster at five twelve.

Questions are best based on information, and Heimrich, late into the case, had less of it than he could have wished when, with Sergeant Forniss, he waited for the five twelve on the station platform. He knew that Constance Gray was twenty years, at least, younger than her husband; that Martin Gray had retired three years before at the age of fifty-five from what appeared to have been a lucrative insurance business; that he had been a widower for some ten years when he remarried and that Mary, who had just passed seventeen, was his only child. Heimrich also knew what Gray, dying, had found strength to say to Professor Brinkley.

Heimrich would have liked more to go on as he watched a pretty blonde woman in a powder blue spring suit come down the steps of a coach of the five twelve. A policeman must, however, go on what he has.

If the pretty blonde woman, with piquant face and wide blue eyes, had driven her car across the road—on the "wrong side"—to kill her husband, there was nothing in her face to show it. Her face was gay. Her hair was immaculately in place. Probably what she had gone to New York for, Heimrich thought, moving toward her. To have her hair done. "Mrs. Gray?" he said, and she stopped. She looked up at two solid men, and her wide eyes widened.

"State Police," Heimrich said, and watched her face, and her face told him. There could be no doubt her face told him, her eyes told him. Constance Gray was afraid. Because they were policemen, she was afraid. It was as easy as that—and, for an instant, Heimrich realized that, watching her, pretty and gay-faced, he had wished it wouldn't be.

"Oh!" she said, as if her breath caught, and then again, "Oh!" And then, which was quite unbelievable, "I knew I should have reported it. I really did know that. But it didn't seem to hurt him."

Heimrich is used to remarkable statements, particularly by murderers. He could remember none more remarkable than this. Here was a woman who had guided a car across a road so as to kill her husband with it, and who said now that she should have reported this—should "really" have reported. And—that being killed hadn't seemed to hurt.

He looked down at her in disbelief. He felt his face falling open, human astonishment triumphing over professional detachment. He pulled his face together. He said, "What are you talking about, Mrs. Gray?" and his voice sounded hard in his own ears.

She looked bewildered then. He had seen that expression on many faces.

"The deer?" she said. "Isn't it about the deer?"

So that was it. One had to give her credit. But not too much.

"It's not about a deer," Heimrich said, and told her flatly what it was about. She began to tremble, then, and put her hands over her face and did (Heimrich thought without sympathy) such other things as she thought appropriate. They took her home, then, to the big white house on Hayride Lane. There her step-daughter ran into her arms and clung to her, and Constance Gray, her own face set, seemed to try to comfort the girl. A very competent actress, Heimrich thought of Constance Gray.

After she had had time enough, she pushed the girl away, gently, then turned to Heimrich and said, in a quite level voice, "Tell me about it, please." Heimrich told her, but not that her husband had died saying her name—part of her name. There would be time for that, later. She said, "You think I—" and then, "How can you think that?" And this, too, was appropriate enough.

"Now, Mrs. Gray," Heimrich said. "I don't think anything yet, naturally." (Which was not really true.) "You didn't see your husband on the road? Didn't run into him? By accident, naturally."

She had not seen Martin Gray—not after they left the house at about the same time, he for his walk, she in the car. He had started north on the left side of the road, and had waved at her. She had driven north to Brewster. There had been a little fog.

"Why do you think—?" she said, and again did not finish, but instead said, "I loved him. We loved each other." And her voice shook at that.

Heimrich waited. Then he said. "You hit a deer? That's how your fender was dented?"

"Yes," she said. "I hit a deer. Only a deer. Is it any use to tell you?"

"Now, Mrs. Gray," Heimrich said. "It's of use, naturally."

She had been two or three miles on the road to Brewster. The fog had lifted. She had not been driving fast. The deer came out of nowhere in one great leap—a big deer, which scrambled and slid on the road surface. "Afterwards," she said, "there was froth on my windshield." She had braked, skidded a little, felt the jar as the car struck him.

"He half fell," she said. "But then he didn't fall. He leaped away—up the bank and away. He didn't seem hurt."

But her voice seemed to die away as she told of the deer. It was, Heimrich thought, as if she lost faith in her story even as she told it. Yet it was not, intrinsically, an improbable story. Few motorists drive long in Northern Westchester without narrowly missing—or not missing—deer charging across roadways. If deer and car survive, there is nothing to report to authority. Then, why the tableau of guilt on the station platform? Explanation of a guilt reaction which could not wholly be concealed? Probably. Of course, the Grays had not lived long in deer country.

A telephone rang in another room. The call was, the maid came to say, for Miss Mary. "That boy—the Beale boy," she said, in a certain tone. The pretty girl, pretty for all the redness of her eyes, ran out of the room.

Constance Gray watched her, and Constance's eyes narrowed a little. She turned back to Heimrich and said, "Her—boy friend. Martin and I are rather—" and stopped with that, and put her hands over her eyes. After a time she took them down and said that she was sorry, and that she was all right now.

"Why do you think it wasn't merely a—a dreadful accident?" she asked him, and her voice was steady.

It was time to tell her, then, and Heimrich told her what her husband had said, dying. Her blue eyes seemed to darken as she listened. And, Heimrich thought, fear grew in them.

"He said, '*No, Con,*'" she repeated, when she had heard. "That was it? As if—as if it were, '*Don't, Con!*' That's what you think?"

There was no need to answer.

"And," she said, "'*Wrong side.*' And I would have been on the wrong side to him. That's it, too?"

"Now, Mrs. Gray,' Heimrich said.

"Because he was older?" she said. "That's what you think? Or—just for the money. The insurance? Double indemnity for accidental death. You'll find that out." She had begun to speak very rapidly. "A hundred thousand dollars," she said. "To kill Martin for. To—"

Suddenly, she began to say, "No. No. No . . ." over and over, as if she would never stop.

Mary Gray ran back into the room, then, and looked at Heimrich with anger. "Go away!" the girl said, in the voice of youth's angry rebellion. "Go away. Leave her alone!"

Heimrich nodded to Sergeant Forniss, and the two tall, solid men did as the girl said, since hysteria is inarticulate, and since Heimrich needed to know more before he could ask more. He did not say that they would be back, since there is no point in saying what is obvious.

Heimrich did know more the next morning, had more to go on, as he drove toward the Gray house—Constance Gray's house now—at a little after eight. He knew that the insurance money went to Constance Gray, along with a good deal more money.

He knew that Martin Gray had been popular enough, certainly had had no "enemies." If one did not count young Rodney Beale, high school senior, who had done some muttering about people who thought they were better than other people because they had a lot of money. (The point apparently being that Martin Gray had considered Rodney, eighteen and a part-time grocery clerk, an unsuitable husband for his daughter.) But boys of eighteen often mutter against fusty parents who have themselves forgotten love.

He was abruptly distracted from his sorting of information. A car came briskly toward him, and the car had no driver. No driver at all! It had a passenger, sitting at the right of the driver's seat. There was nobody behind the wheel.

Heimrich's car winced toward the side of the road. But then the approaching car swerved abruptly to the right and stopped beside a rural mail box. Heimrich laughed, soundlessly, at himself.

A good many rural route men drove in that fashion, needing only a car with automatic transmission—sat on the wrong side, but the side nearest boxes, drove with left hand and foot, and so avoided much sliding across seats to take mail out of boxes and to poke it in. All the same, it was somewhat alarming to see when a car so driven came head on. And all the same, it was rather risky. In an emergency, a man on the wrong side of the driver's seat wouldn't have much control. Not much con...

Wrong side, No con—wrong side of the *car*, not of the *road!*

Heimrich drove on, but not to the big white house he had been headed for. He drove to another house like it, but half a mile north on Hayride Lane. He said to the gray-haired man there, "When Mr. Gray said 'con' and stopped, did it sound like an emphasized first syllable? As if he might have been going to say '*Con*stance?' or—"

"I've been worrying about that," Professor Brinkley said in a worried voice. "I was afraid they would think I was just being—fussy. Unemphasized, I'm quite sure. The indeterminate sound of the vowel, you know. And—"

"Yes," Heimrich said, "as if he really meant to say control."

Heimrich drove into North Wellwood, then, and to the small cottage where Thomas Beale, driver of rural route no. 2, lived with his wife. Not that Beale would be there; he would be on the route. But—

Beale was there. His wife said so. In bed with one of his migraines. And had been the day before. And—

"Tom's nephew is taking the route for him," Mrs. Beale said and was anxious, and twisted her apron in her hands. "Rod, that is. There isn't anything wrong, is there?"

"I hope not," Heimrich said going as far as he could go. He drove two blocks to another cottage, where the Whitney Beales lived with their son, Rodney, but he did not go to the door. He waited in his car for an hour or more before Rodney Beale, driving as his uncle drove—as what boy of eighteen would not, given an excuse?—turned into the driveway.

He was a big boy. All the same, his instinct was to run. Heimrich could see that in his tense body, his working, frightened face.

"Well, son?" Heimrich said.

"I didn't mean to," the boy said. "He just sort of stumbled out in front of me and—I— He was dead. I couldn't do anything. Wasn't he dead?"

"No," Heimrich said. "I don't say it would have made any difference if you'd got help. But—he wasn't dead."

"Nobody would have believed me," the boy said. "After— I've been saying things about him. And—"

"We might have," Heimrich said. "We might still. But— you'll have to come with me now, son."

A boy can panic, Heimrich thought, driving away from the Brewster substation of the New York State Police. Anybody can panic. Probably the boy hadn't meant to kill—not consciously meant to kill. So probably it wasn't actually murder, which is Heimrich's special concern.

Heimrich turned his car into Hayride Lane once more, toward Constance Gray's big white house. There he would have to make what amounted to an apology.

Sources Heimrich Stumbles

SOURCES HEIMRICH STUMBLES

The widow of Paul Winters stood just inside the door of Captain M. L. Heimrich's office in the Troop K barracks at Hawthorne at a little after two o'clock on a Saturday afternoon late in March. She was a slight woman, with a feather of gray in her dark hair. Her eyes were very wide, very shocked. Heimrich wished he could help her, but had no certainty that he could—or that anybody could.

Paul Winters had died violently some four hours earlier. But Heimrich's concern was with homicide and Winters had died in an automobile accident—an accident that had only involved him. It was simple, uncomplicated; already, the troopers assigned to the case had it wrapped up and filed away. It had nothing to do with the Bureau of Criminal Investigation, New York State Police, and hence nothing to do with Captain M. L. Heimrich.

So there was nothing he could do to help the woman whose dark eyes were so wide, so fixed—the woman who looked so much as if she had been cruelly, physically, and, above all, unexpectedly struck in the face.

Ten minutes before she came into his office, Heimrich had been sitting at his desk, involved in other matters. The telephone had rung and he had picked it up and said, "Heimrich." He listened, then said, "What's the name again?" since he had not heard the name before. He listened further. Finally he said, "Why, if it's accidental?" but then, after a moment more, he murmured, "All right. That's what we're here for. But let me have the report first. Then the lady."

The report came. He looked at it. A man—name of Winters, Paul—had lost control of his car on a friend's driveway. The car had pitched down a steep slope, hit a low retaining wall, landed upside down in ten feet of water. Tossed in the car, Winters had struck his head on something—the sharp corner of an opened ashtray probably—and so had been unconscious when he drowned. But he would not have been able to escape, in any case, since both doors had jammed when the car crashed.

Winters, presumably, had lost control of his car—as many others had that morning—because he was driving through a blinding snowstorm. Heimrich looked up from the accident report and out of his office window. Snow was still falling, although not so heavily now.

It had been very bad that morning, when Heimrich had driven cautiously down to Hawthorne from Van Brunt Center. "Hazardous driving conditions," his car radio told him, needlessly. It was no great consolation to learn, at the same time, that in Manhattan it was merely raining. It had been merely raining when Paul Winters set out that morning from Manhattan, where he lived, to visit a Mr. Bertram Smith, his partner in business (importing), who had recently bought a riverside house near North Salem.

It was Smith who had reported the accident to the police. The accident had occurred on the steep, twisting driveway down to Smith's house. Winters's car had skidded off into Smith's small lake, made by damming a little river, and it was there that Paul Winters had died.

So—a fatal accident. An accident properly investigated, duly reported on. But Paul Winters's widow insisted on seeing Captain Heimrich.

Heimrich lifted his telephone again and said, "All right. Ask Mrs. Winters to come in, please." Then he stood up, a large and solid man, with very blue eyes in a square face.

Somebody in the anteroom opened the door for Mrs. Paul Winters and she stepped into Heimrich's office and somebody closed the door behind her. She was crying, and did not seem to know that she was crying. When she spoke, her voice was very low—so low that Heimrich had to strain to hear her words.

"I had to see someone," she said. "Someone who—who could tell me. Who *would* tell me. I'd—something I heard about you made me think you would. I don't remember who said—" She stopped speaking. Then she whispered, "I can't seem to stop crying." It was as if she spoke to herself.

Heimrich went around the desk and did not touch the slender woman, but he spoke very gently and got her to sit in a wooden chair across from his desk; he did not look at, but saw, her hands twisting a handkerchief. Then Heimrich went back to his own chair and held out a pack of cigarettes toward her. She did not seem to see it.

"Captain Heimrich," she said, "I have to know. Paul—my husband—wanted to die, didn't he? I mean—he killed himself. Isn't that true? You don't want to tell me and I—I understand that. You think it wouldn't do any good, wouldn't make any difference. The others—they're just trying to be kind. That's it, isn't it?"

"Killed himself?" Heimrich repeated. "Why do you say that, Mrs. Winters?"

"Then he did," she said, and covered her face with frail hands as her whole body shook. She spoke in so low a tone that, with her hands muffling the sound, Heimrich could not be wholly sure what she said. But then he was sure. "It's my fault," she said, behind the screening hands. "My fault. My—"

"Mrs. Winters," Heimrich said, "Listen to me. There's nothing—nothing at all—to suggest your husband killed himself. Everything to show it was an accident. There were many traffic accidents this morning."

He took her hands down from her face. Her eyes still had the startled look, the look of shocked surprise.

"Mrs. Winters," Heimrich said, speaking very slowly. "I want you to listen to me. There is nothing—*nothing at all*—to suggest that this was anything but an accident. The troopers who went there are good men, trained men. If there had been anything suspicious—"

He stopped. She did not seem to be listening.

"You don't understand," she said, and it was clear she had not been listening to Heimrich, but only to her own thoughts. She spoke toward him, not to him. "It was up to me to see—that he did not die. The doctor said that. As good as said that. A few months—six months perhaps—and Paul would be himself again. He said it was almost always like that when—when the case was simple. As he said Paul's was. What I had to do was see that he didn't die."

She put her hands over her face again and Heimrich waited. "Didn't kill himself," she said. " 'It's up to his friends'—that's what the doctor said. 'Most of all, of course, it's up to you.' To me. *Me*."

Again her body began to shake. There was nothing Heimrich could do about that. He waited, and gradually she grew quieter. She took her hands away from her face and looked at him. Her eyes had not changed. "I have to know whether I failed," she said. "Whether I have to live with that. I—*I have to know*."

A policeman needs to have a smattering of many kinds of knowledge; he needs such a smattering to detect patterns.

"Your husband had been in a depression?" Heimrich said. "Had been seeing a psychiatrist?"

She nodded. She was crying again, and paid no attention to the tears on her face.

"And," she said, "protection. Protection from—himself. Do you understand now?"

Heimrich did. A man, almost himself again, not quite himself again, entrusted to tenderness and—watchfulness. The swings between depression and elation shortened, the periods of equilibrium, of normality, growing longer. But—the moments of mind's darkness still occurring. In which—She was, of course, quite right. She might have failed. Failure might have been inevitable, guiltless.

He looked at the slender woman. It would do no good to tell her that.

Because Paul Winters might well have taken this way to kill himself when darkness settled on his mind. There was no point in denying that to the shaken woman. She would have to live with that—live, at the best, with the possibility of that; with a question which could not Heimrich supposed, ever be answered. At least, he saw no way to answer it.

But she waited—waited for an answer.

"Mr. Winters had been ill for some time?" Heimrich asked, not seeing that the answer to that would lead to any other answer.

He had been. For about a year he had been under psychiatric treatment in a private hospital. Two weeks ago he had been discharged as much improved, ready to try for the adjustment which he would have to make. But released with a proviso— always with a proviso.

"He seemed quite himself," his widow said and now— although Heimrich thought the effort was great for her—she spoke steadily. "Until yesterday."

The day before he had gone to his business office for the first time. And when he came home, she thought he was upset. He denied it, laughing at her gently, saying she must quit worrying about him. He admitted he was a little tired. That was all. Taking hold again after so long a time away was, naturally, tiring. That was all.

"The doctor," she said, "told me not to be—to be *too* protective. Not to let him feel that I didn't trust him or was worrying about him too much."

Winters had told his wife that he was driving up the next morning to see Bert. If he could find Bert's new house. "Bertram Smith," she said. "His partner." Heimrich nodded. "He said something about there being a business point or two he wanted to clear up with Bert. I tried to talk him out of it, but he laughed at me. Said he'd already made the date with Bert and—"

Unexpectedly she broke down and her body shook again.

"I had an appointment," she said. "An appointment to have my hair done. *To have my hair done.* So—I let him go alone. For nothing more than that! To have my—" Once more she covered her face with her hands. She moved her head slowly from side to side. Heimrich could only wait. There wasn't anything to say. She steadied herself again, and again it was painful to watch the effort.

"You see now," she said. "I have to know. You do see that? If—if Paul killed himself, if I failed him, I have to know. *One way or the other.* You can live with a thing you know—some way you can—" she paused. "But I have to know."

And saying that, she laid the problem in Heimrich's hands, laid the impossible in his hands. Because there was no way, there never would be any way, of knowing. Accident or intention? The <reason> was the same, and the answer was lost forever in a mind snapped off.

"I'll do what I can," Heimrich heard himself say. "I can't promise anything."

She would wait for him—was there. No matter how long it would take. "I've nothing else to do," she said. "Nothing to do anywhere."

Heimrich drove north and east. The plows had not yet got to the township road which he turned into beyond North Salem, and when he turned from that onto the private road which served three widely separated houses—one of them Bertram Smith's—the surface was a churned-up mess. Churned up, Heimrich supposed, by policemen who had been there before him—been there when there was possibly something to find out.

The private road, narrow and twisting, had been staked— staked for winter guidance in snow, and left staked into late March, with a pessimism that events had fully justified. The stakes were driven on either side of the road, at intervals of twenty feet or so, and marked the road's course. A little-traveled road can disappear in heavy snow.

The road dead-ended in a turnaround beyond a sign which just protruded above the snow and was lettered "Bertram Smith." Heimrich stopped his car in the turnaround and walked back.

Winters could not, Heimrich thought—looking down the driveway—merely have missed the turn. The driveway was staked as the road had been—round, green stakes, dahlia stakes, driven in on both sides and about twenty feet apart. Even driving through heavily falling snow, as Winters had been, he could hardly have failed to see the guiding stakes.

So—he had skidded off the roadway.

Or—he had deliberately turned off it, seeking death.

The drive was rutted. Police cars had crept up and down it; an ambulance had gone down empty and climbed back, not empty.

Heimrich walked down in the ruts to the twist in the drive. He did not expect to find anything the troopers had missed—he did not expect to find anything at all. Even if the car had skidded, even if it had left skid marks, nothing would be proved. A car turned sharply on a slippery surface is likely to skid.

The marks the car had made in snow and earth went straight down to the river. The marks would tell him nothing—they had already told nothing to the troopers, beyond what was obvious. Nevertheless, as he started down the slope toward the battered car—hauled out of the water now, a wreck by the water's edge—Heimrich did not walk in the tracks, but through unmarked snow beside them. If there *was* anything to be discovered, there was no use in trampling it out.

Halfway down, shuffling carefully through the snow, Heimrich stumbled. He flailed the air, seeking balance, not finding it on the slope. Captain Heimrich fell—not quite flat on his face, since he broke his fall with outstretched hands, but flat enough. He swore, got up, brushed himself off. Of all the awkward damn things to do—

He went back to see what he had stumbled over. He squatted down and brushed the snow aside. He had stumbled over the broken end of a green stake which protruded three or four inches from the ground into which—*into which it had been driven*.

Heimrich then sat back on his heels and stared at nothing. After a time he said, just audibly, that he would be damned.

He rose and walked on, very slowly, down the slope, his eyes on the ground. He found what he was looking for—a place where the snow had been disturbed. He squatted again and, carefully, brushed the snow aside. Again he found what he was looking for—a neat, round hole through turf, into clayey earth. This stake had come out clean when it was pulled out, had not broken off as the other stake—the other lying stake— had broken. There would be more holes, without doubt, where the other stakes had been pulled from clinging earth. But they could be looked for later.

Heimrich went back to the drive and began to walk down it toward the house—toward the house and a man who had known Paul Winters was driving up that morning, and had wanted Winters dead; toward, it was almost inevitable, a man named Bertram Smith, since who else could have switched the stakes in Smith's front yard and not been caught at it? Switched them to guide a car off an unfamiliar road and to almost certain death. Switched them to kill. Hence, a murderer and one who, murder achieved, had merely to pull up the lying stakes and put them back where they should be—where they must be found later, along the driveway's true edges, telling the truth again.

And by then, a murderer in a hurry—in such a hurry that he had broken one of the stakes he wrenched at and had to leave the three-or-four-inch stump in the ground—broken it off so that enough remained above ground to make a policeman, seeking something else, stumble on murder. He would have needed to hurry. The crash of the car against the retaining wall might well have been heard, so the accident had to be reported quickly. There had been also, of course, the need to cover foot-marks he had left in the snow as he went from stake to stake, pulling them out. A broom would start that and the thickly falling snow would finish it. Still, there had been a need to work fast—too fast, as it had turned out.

What Paul Winters, on his first visit to his business office in a year, had discovered was anybody's guess. Certainly something Smith could not let go further. Theft of some kind probably. They would have to find out.

There was much that remained to be found out, to be organized, to be proved. There might be difficulties; Smith was clearly an ingenious man—a most ingenious man. But now that they knew what had happened, now that they knew what to look for—

Heimrich stopped going down the drive, stood for a moment, then turned back. Smith—in his house or not—would keep a few minutes longer.

Heimrich went back to his car and used the two-way radio to call the barracks. He could do nothing for Paul Winters now, except catch his murderer. But he might, with what he had to tell her, help an anguished woman go on living, help her pick up the pieces—he could, at any rate, free her from the agony of guilt.

Which was not much; which was something . . .

IF THEY GIVE HIM TIME

IF THEY GIVE HIM TIME

Beyond the open casement windows of the Myron Drake house in Oak Hill, the night breathed softly, slowly, of heavy air. The shrill, endlessly repeated notes of a whippoorwill's cry slashed through the sound of the dog-day cicadas.

Captain M. L. Heimrich, New York State Police, said, "Thank you, Mr. Burnett," to a stocky man in his mid-forties. "We appreciate your help."

Jason Brunett stood up. He hesitated. "I hope this doesn't get the boy in trouble," he said. "But—I hadn't any alternative." He still hesitated—waited, Heimrich realized to be reassured.

"No alternative," Heimrich said, giving him the answer he waited for. "Nothing else you could do, naturally. Not when it's murder."

Burnett nodded his head slowly, unhappily. He walked across the living room toward the door. He limped rather badly. "By the way," Heimrich said, "do you mind waiting while we talk to the boy?"

Burnett shook his head and limped to the door.

"All right," Heimrich said to Sergeant Charles Forniss. "We'll talk to the boy, now." Forniss went into another room and came back with Ned Drake, who had found his father murdered some two hours before. Or said he had. He had quarreled violently with his father earlier in the evening. Or Jason Burnett, who had been his father's business partner, said he had. Burnett said he had been out in the kitchen making himself a drink and had stayed during the entire quarrel. That was what he felt he had to tell.

Ned Drake had soft, pale hair which seemed to shine in the lamplight. His lips twitched a little. A boy still, Heimrich thought—a boy for all that he was twenty-one, and a husband of three weeks. A slender, nervous, good-looking boy.

"Tell me what happened," Heimrich said. "Beginning with this quarrel you had with your father, this quarrel about your wife. At a little after eight this evening, Mr. Burnett says it was."

The boy sat down. He put slender hands in front of his face, as if light hurt his eyes. He nodded his head, slowly, his face still screened.

"Dad was dead when I got here," Ned Drake said. "Lying on the floor with his head—" He did not finish; a long shudder ran through his slim body.

Heimrich waited, knowing what the slug from a .45 can do to the human head. After a time, he prompted. "The quarrel, Mr. Drake? About your wife?"

"Dad said she was no good," the boy said. "After money. Nothing else. That wasn't true. Not about Doris. She's . . ." But he did not finish.

It took time, patience. The quarrel was not denied. Perhaps he had blown up a little, the boy admitted. Not because of what his father threatened, which was to cut off his allowance if he didn't leave the girl. But because of what Myron Drake had said to his son about the girl. "Nasty things," the boy said. "I told him what he could do with his money . . ."

But again he trailed off. Heimrich gave him more time.

Ned Drake had told his father what he could do with the money, and had gone back to the Old Stone Inn in Van Brunt to tell his new wife—his eighteen-year-old wife—what had come of it. And he had found his wife gone, packed up and gone. He had telephoned a few places. Then he had walked back from the inn to his father's house. He had got there about eleven and found his father dead. That was all he knew.

"Why did you come back?" Heimrich asked. "To tell your father he was right, after all? That you'd take the money and let the lady go? Since she had gone in any case?"

Heimrich watched the boy. He should flare at that. Ned Drake did not flare. A licked boy, Heimrich thought.

"Or—to pay him off?" Heimlich said. "Was that it? Because you hated him for being right? Killed him for being right?"

"He was dead when I got here," the boy said. "Didn't somebody say he was shot at a quarter of eleven? Didn't somebody say that? I was a mile from here then."

There was no doubt that Myron Drake had been shot at a quarter of eleven. A good many living in the Oak Hill development—place of trees and curving roads and bright new houses, each on its own two acres—had heard the shot. Several had looked at their clocks.

A man named Harry Simpkins, Jason Burnett's next door neighbor, had been walking his dog and had heard the shot plainly, had looked at his watch and could swear to the time. Every night at 10:30 he took the dog out and walked him for half an hour. "Like clockwork," Harry Simpkins said. "You can set your watch by me and old Duke." The shot had sounded at 10:45.

But nobody, except the boy himself, could swear that Ned Drake had been a mile away when his father died, and not in the room with a gun—Myron Drake's own gun, it had been—in his hand and hatred in his heart.

"Damn it!" the boy said, with sudden violence. "He was dead when I got here, I tell you—"

But Sergeant Forniss stood in a doorway and the boy stopped. "Yes Charlie?" Heimrich said, and Forniss said, "The girl's here, captain. Mrs. Drake."

"No!" Ned Drake said. "Don't drag her—"

"All right, Charlie," Heimrich said. "Ask Mrs. Drake to come in."

She came in. Heimrich had supposed she would be pretty, and she was pretty. She had dark red hair, she was delicately made, as the boy was. But she seemed, standing in the room, to be made of silver wires. And that Heimrich had expected.

"What are they doing to you?" she said to the boy, to her husband. But she spoke as to a boy. He looked up at her.

"You came back," he said, "or—they brought you back. That was it, wasn't it?"

She looked at him, and shook her head a little. She turned to Heimrich and turned (Heimrich thought) as one adult to another. But she was eighteen and her face was very young. "What are you doing to him?" she said to Heimrich.

"Asking him questions," Heimrich said. "About murder. But you know that, Mrs. Drake."

"You're crazy," she said. She did not speak with the accents of the Hudson Valley, as the boy. That would have made a difference to Myron Drake, Heimrich supposed. "He was with me," the girl said. "In our room." She was very young, very defiant.

Heimrich closed his eyes for a moment and shook his head. She looked at the boy. She said, "Didn't you tell him that?"

"It's no good, Doris," the boy said, and spoke in a dull voice. "I didn't kill Dad. But he knows we weren't together."

She looked at Heimrich. Her eyes were as blue as Heimrich's. There seemed to be fire behind them.

"Yes," Heimrich said. "Your husband says he went back from here to the inn at about nine, or a little after, and found you gone. He tried to find you and then walked back here. But you say he was with you?"

"That's no good, is it?" the girl said, with odd acceptance. But she wasn't licked—not she. "Worth trying, was all."

"Yes," Heimrich said.

"Oh," the girl said. "I don't blame you. Not you. Only, he couldn't kill anybody. His father would say, 'Put it down son,' and he'd put it down. Put *anything* down." She was bitter, with that.

The boy said, "Doris—"

She made a gesture. It was as if, in words, she told him to keep out of this.

"Mr. Burnett," she said suddenly. "You've thought about Mr. Burnett?"

"Why?" Heimrich said. (He had, and it had got him nowhere.)
"Why Mr. Burnett?"

The girl looked at Ned Drake. Her eyes demanded.

"Mr. Burnett and Dad were insured in each other's favor," the boy said. "I suppose she means that."

"Well?" The girl said to Heimrich.

Heimrich shook his head. "Mr. Burnett was at home," he said. "In his kitchen. Getting himself a snack, he says."

"He says," the girl repeated, but Heimrich shook his head again. It was more than that. Burnett had been seen there, or as good as seen. By the man named Simpkins—the man walking his dog, as he did every night.

Simpkins had just stepped onto his terrace when a light went on in Burnett's kitchen. And it was 10:30 then. He could swear to that time, and to the time of the shot, fifteen, minutes later. And he could swear that the light in Burnett's kitchen went off five minutes after the shot. Simpkins had thought somebody was shooting at a woodchuck, at first.

"In the middle of the night," the girl said, with derision.

Simpkins had remembered that woodchucks hole up at night—remembered that later. Then he had gone to Burnett's to see what Burnett made of it. There was no one there. Burnett, who lived alone in the house, had heard the shot, too—heard it, he said, while he was in the kitchen, in pajamas, a glass of milk in his hand. He had not thought of woodchucks, but of a quarrel in a house half a mile away—a quarrel and a boy's violent words.

Burnett had dressed and walked slowly to Drake's house—walked because his car was in a service garage for a tune-up; walked slowly because that was the only way he had to walk. The police had got there before he did, but not by much.

"Somebody else, then," the girl said. "Not Ned. Somebody who broke in?"

"Perhaps," Heimrich said. (But there was nothing to indicate anybody had broken in, or tried to.) "All right," he said.

"We'll go on with it tomorrow." He looked at his watch. "Later today," he said. They were surprised, which was all right with Heimrich. It was to be supposed that, left to it, they would put their heads together. Heimrich was a man who prized efforts by suspects to embellish. He left them to it.

Jason Burnett had waited. He was sitting in a deck chair on the terrace. Heimrich went across the terrace and Burnett stood up and said, "You didn't need me?"

"No," Heimrich said. "It was the way you said."

"The kid?" Burnett said, and there was distress in his voice. "I hoped he'd—" Burnett did not finish. Heimrich said it looked like the kid. Burnett's shoulders slumped. He took a few limping steps.

"I'll run you home," Heimrich said.

It was only minutes in a police car to the neat, small—but very modern—house Jason Burnett lived in, and had lived alone in since his wife died. "A nightcap?" Burnett said, when the car stopped. Heimrich hesitated, decided he could do with something long and cold.

Burnett turned on lights and limped across the living room to the kitchen. Heimrich went along.

The kitchen shone very white. Heimrich looked around it while Burnett got ice from a big refrigerator. A lot of equipment for a man living alone—freezer and electric range, dishwasher, automatic laundry. "I've got the place on the market," Burnett said. "Not much good to me—not now."

There was a wide window over the range. Heimrich looked out into darkness.

"Wouldn't think the Simpkins were so close, would you?" Burnett said, standing beside him. "A good thing for me they are, isn't it?" He looked at Heimrich. "And," he said "that Harry was walking his dog just then." He smiled faintly and sipped his drink. "Might have got ideas otherwise, mightn't you?"

"Now, Mr. Burnett," Heimrich said, and put his drink down on the convenient range. "You're thinking of the insurance—"

And then he stopped, and leaned down, and Burnett looked at him curiously.

"Cooking something tonight, Mr. Burnett?" Heimrich said. "Not this morning, obviously. You were in the city this morning. At—" He leaned down and looked again at the many dials and buttons of the automatic range. "At about ten minutes of eleven?"

Heimrich did not look at Burnett. Only at the range.

"To be finished cooking at ten of eleven," Heimrich said. "After cooking twenty minutes. It's set that way. To go on, then, at ten-thirty. And—not the oven. Not one of the top burners." He pointed at the row of buttons which selected the unit to be used automatically. "The outlet," Heimrich said, and pointed at the one he meant—the plug-in receptacle in the headboard of the range; the one marked "AUTO."

"Making coffee tonight, Mr. Burnett? Or—*turning on a light?* A lamp plugged into the outlet? To go on at ten-thirty, when Mr. Simpkins walks his dog every night? Like clockwork, he says. And, off at ten to eleven, with your partner dead? How much is the insurance, Mr. Burnett?"

Burnett stared at the stove—not at Heimrich. At the stove.

"Yes," Heimrich said. "We all make mistakes. Forgot to reset it, didn't you? Put the lamp back where you got it. But forgot all about the stove controls." He made a sound with tongue and teeth, a sound almost of sympathy. Then he said he'd use Mr. Burnett's telephone, if Mr. Burnett didn't mind. And Burnett began to swear and seemed, absurdly enough, to be swearing at an automatic electric range.

Jason Burnett was on his way to Carmel, County of Putnam, State of New York, and conversation with an assistant district attorney. Heimrich would join them there, but first there was a message to be delivered. He walked across the grass toward the Drake house, where windows stood open and lights still burned.

He could not see the boy and girl inside the living room, but he could hear them clearly.

"—whatever you're told," the girl said. "Like a child. Your father says, 'Cut off the money and watch her go. The little gold digger.' Oh, I don't know the words. Not the words he'd use. Very smooth words, probably. And you—"

"Please, Doris," the boy said. "Please listen to me."

"What I'm like," she said. "You wouldn't know that, would you? Just what Papa tells you. 'Yes, Papa. I guess she is, Papa.' Like a little boy. Like a little, *little* boy."

"You left. Took your things."

"Baby," she said. "Oh—baby." There was something near a sob in her young voice. "You thought," she said, "that I'd just wait there to be told? That I didn't know already? Know that whatever Papa said—" She broke off. It was easy to guess why. "No," the girl said. "That's not enough, Ned. Not now. Come back—come back when you grow up." There was another moment and then, again, she said, "No. Ned," and then, "Oh, I love you. Damn it and damn it. But—when you grow up."

It was seconds before Ned Drake spoke, and then he spoke, slowly, in a voice Heimrich had not heard him use before. "All right," Ned Drake said. "I'll—I'll try, Doris. If they let me. If they give me time."

Heimrich scuffled his feet on the flagstones and knocked, so that he could go in and tell a boy that time was his, for all "they" had to do with it. Heimrich found himself hoping, and rather believing, the boy would use it well—with the girl to help. There had to be something to a boy who would pick a girl like that. It would be interesting, Heimrich thought, to see which of them came to open the door to him, not knowing yet what was to be faced.

Ned Drake opened the door. He stood straight and looked at Heimrich steadily, and waited.

Heimrich smiled, nodded his head a little, and then told Ned Drake what he had come to tell him.

CAT OF DREAMS

Ann Notson was nine years old; she had eyes which in certain lights looked green; there was a kind of glow in her soft brown hair. Her mother had had such eyes and hair, and so Philip Notson, when he looked at his daughter, must often—too often—have been reminded of his wife.

Ann Notson was an imaginative child—a "very" imaginative child, her teacher in Van Brunt District School had written, underlining the word "very." This, decided Captain M. L. Heimrich of the New York State Police, meant that Ann sometimes saw things which were not there or, perhaps, saw what was there in a more interesting form than was entirely real.

There was, however, no doubt of the very ugly reality of what she saw at about eight-thirty of a bright, cold Saturday morning in mid-December—saw behind the garage of her father's house on Brickhouse Road in the town of Van Brunt, County of Putnam. She had gone out of the house to find a "kitty." "May I be excused, please?" she said to her father, who was lingering over breakfast coffee, as a man may on Saturday morning. "I want to go out and see if the kitty is all right."

"Um-mm," Philip Notson said. "Bundle up, kitten." He heard the front door slam and stopped, coffee cup halfway between saucer and lips, and expression drained out of his eyes. It was the little meaningless things which now were the worst things. Jean had always closed doors more firmly than necessary.... He wrenched his mind from memory.

What "kitty" did Ann expect to find? A cat of dreams, probably, since they had no cat; a "kitty" who frisked, chased his tail, only in a child's quick mind.

He picked up the newspaper. He made himself read it.

The door slammed again. She hadn't stayed long. No kitty to be found, he supposed. However imaginative a child . . .

"Daddy," Ann said, almost before she was in the dining room. *"Daddy!* There's a man out there. Lying right on the ground. Is he asleep, Daddy? Because it's cold. It's—*awful* cold."

There was urgency in the clear voice; there was something— fear? shock?—in the child's greenish eyes. Philip Notson said, "Where?" and, on being told, went to see. The man who lay on the ground behind the garage, between it and the bank which broke sharply down from the field above, was not asleep.

Captain Heimrich, whose chief concern was with mur- der, drove up the driveway from Brickhouse Road to Philip Notson's white and gray house at a little after nine. Fortunately he had been nearby.

There were police cars already in the driveway and in the turnaround in front of the garage. He went around the garage and looked down at the body of Malcolm Arthur Bell.

Just two days before, on Thursday, Heimrich had heard Bell called "a very fortunate man" by County Judge Davies, who had just accepted a verdict of Not Guilty from a jury in the Carmel courthouse. Not guilty, that was, of manslaughter in connection with the death of one Jean Notson, thirty-one years old, at about one thirty-five o'clock on the morning of Sunday, the twenty-first of September. Bell's luck had now run out.

"Oh," Philip Notson said to Heimrich. "I see how it looks. He killed my wife. The jury says he's not guilty of anything. And—I said some bitter things and was heard saying them. I see how it looks. All the same—"

All the same, he knew nothing of Bell's death. Murder, if they were so sure it was that. He himself had thought that Bell had stumbled on the rough steps leading down from the upper field, pitched headlong, and landed on a rock. Which, he said with some savagery, would have been appropriate.

Heimrich, a notably stolid man, sat and watched and lis- tened to Philip Notson—a slim, quick man, tall and with just a suggestion of the tall man's stoop. Notson walked back and forth in the living room and made quick motions with his hands. He was in his middle thirties; his hair was beginning to recede a little; the summer's tan had not quite faded from his mobile face.

"No," Heimrich said, "he didn't fall, Mr. Notson. He was struck. Several times, probably with an iron bar. Sometime yesterday evening. Between five and nine, at a guess—a wide guess, admittedly. He would have come that way, coming here?"

"Across the field? Yes. They used to. He and his wife. Not since Jean died. Since—he killed her."

But it had not been like that—not as Phil Notson said it now, looking down, his eyes angry, at Heimrich. The jury had said it was an accident—an accident in the early hours of a Sunday morning, after a dance.

"Come on and ride in a real car," Mal Bell had said to Jean Notson, a pretty, slender woman in a gray-green party dress, and patted the hood of his sports car. "Just try it and you'll make old stick-in-the-mud get you one."

They had all laughed, not that there was anything especially funny, but because they were young enough, and gay, and had had a good time at the country club dance.

They had all had drinks, but nobody—and specifically, of course, Malcolm Bell—had had too many. Bell said that it was a blown front tire that sent the hurrying little car into a tree, and Jean out of the car—far, far out of it, until a stone fence stopped her diving flight.

"As to yesterday evening, Mr. Notson," Heimrich said. "You got home about when?"

"A little after seven."Heimrich raised his eyebrows and waited. Van Brunt is an express-train hour from Grand Central. Most commuters manage to make the 5:06.   , .

Notson had missed the usual train, he told Heimrich. He had telephoned Mrs. Billings, who was the housekeeper, and caught the 5:58. Heimrich could ask Mrs. Billings. "Oh," Heimrich said. "Yes, naturally. You came home, had dinner. Then?"

"Read to my daughter. Saw she got to bed—about eight thirty. Read a little longer and went to bed myself. Didn't take time out to kill Mal Bell."

Heimrich said, "Now, Mr. Notson," and then Sergeant Forniss opened the door from the hall and made a motion with his head. Heimrich went out into the hall and closed the door behind him.

A little girl, with very wide greenish eyes and very soft brown hair and wearing a snow suit, was sitting on the third step of the stairs which led up from the hall, and looking out through the front door.

Heimrich smiled at her and Ann Notson said, "I saw a man." She had, Heimrich knew. That she would forget seeing him, after time enough, Heimrich hoped. He said, "Yes, dear," and listened to Forniss.

Then he smiled again at the little girl and went back into the living room, and told Philip Notson that the people across the road had seen the floodlight come on at the Notson place about nine o'clock the previous evening, and said that it had stayed on for about a quarter of an hour. Could Mr. Notson—

"Oh," Phil Notson said, and was very quick in speaking. "That. People looking for the Blakes. Live on Van Brunt Lane, the Blakes do. Next road up. They'd turned off too soon. Told them how to get there."

He looked at Heimrich with challenge. Heimrich told Philip Notson that he saw.

"No reason we would have heard anything," Notson said. "Unless Bell shouted. Maybe not even then. We'd have been in the dining room, the kitten—Ann, that is—and I, and Mrs. Billings in the kitchen."

"No," Heimrich said. "Killing that way doesn't make a lot of noise. Well—"

"You know about the Perkins kid?" Notson said. "What Perkins said he'd do?"

"I know," Heimrich said. "We'll talk to Mr. Perkins."

"Kid of twelve," Notson said—"Crippled now. Who knows when he'll walk again? Because a louse doesn't look where he's going, where he's driving his car. The kid was a pitcher."

"I know," Heimrich said. But he also knew, and supposed that Philip Notson knew—but a bitter mind cannot be predicted—that Bell had not been at fault that time, either; that Jimmy Perkins had been on a bicycle, and had wobbled into the road too far, and that Bell had been driving within the limit, which was forty, through the place they called The Flats, and had done all that could be expected of a driver. (Except, possibly, to drive below the posted speed, which was too high, considering the number of kids, and dogs, on the highway where it ran through The Flats.)

The boy's father, a short and powerfully built man who was a yardman for the Van Brunt Supply Company, had said a lot of things which, it was to be presumed, he hadn't meant. At any rate, that had been a year ago and Perkins had not done anything. Except, of course, to collect a modest sum—modest since Bell had done all that could, officially, be asked—from Bell's insurance company.

Heimrich said, "Well, thanks, Mr. Notson," and went out into the hall. Forniss raised his eyebrows in inquiry and Heimrich shrugged in answer.

The little girl was still on the third step. She said, "You're a policeman, aren't you?"

"Yes, Ann," Heimrich said and smiled down at the little girl—the pretty little girl who, they said, looked so much like her mother. "I'm a policeman."

"I saw a man," Ann said. "When I turned the lights on. He was running. And a kitty."

"Yes," Heimrich said, but sat down on his heels so that he was level with the little girl. "Running?"

"A funny man," Ann said. "Thick. He ran funny. Why don't you wear clothes like the other policemen?"

Heimrich explained about that. He said, "When did you see the funny man, Ann?"

She had seen him the previous evening. When it was time for Daddy to come home—Mrs. Billings had said he was going to be late, but you couldn't tell—she turned on the floodlights over the garage. "It's my—perogative." She stopped and looked at Heimrich with doubt. He nodded his head. "Since Mamma went away," Ann said. "So Daddy won't bump into anything."

She had turned the light on at ten minutes after six—"precisely"— and she had seen the funny man running away from the house, toward the road. (He was funny, Heimrich decided, because he was a grown person and was running. Which was quite reasonable.) Ann didn't know who he was. He wasn't Mr. Bell. Of course she knew Mr. Bell. He wasn't Daddy. "Don't be so silly."

"And," Ann Notson said, "there was a kitty. Just where the light stops. It had shiny eyes, like tail lights."

That was unexpected. In semi-darkness, but with light on them, the eyes of cats shine—shine green, shine yellow.

"Like tail lights?" Heimrich said. "How like tail lights, dear?"

"Red," Ann said. "Red as anything. Like in the fireplace sometimes."

"Oh " Heimrich said. "Did you tell Daddy about the kitty with red eyes? And about the man?"

"Of course," Ann said. "He said I shouldn't make up things. Everybody says that." She paused. "All the *time*," she said. "He said cats never have red eyes. But this—"

Heimrich touched the soft brown hair, smiled at her, stood up, and supposed that people did, all the *time*, tell Ann not to make things up.

A man running.

A red-eyed cat.

For a moment Heimrich wished that, just this once at any rate, a cat's eyes would glow red in semi-darkness with a light on them, instead of green or yellow; that, such a glow, and a man running, would prove not to be merely things a little girl had made up. It would be bad for the soft-haired child if something happened to Daddy . . .

Things are collected, are put together. This takes time, since the collection must extend to byways. It takes more men than two. A trooper had been sent to talk to James Perkins, and by no means only to carry out Heimrich's assurance to Philip Notson.

Perkins was to be asked—was asked—whether he still had borne a grudge against the man who had maimed his son. He was also to be asked—was asked—where he had been the previous evening . . . between the hours of five, say, and nine.

The trooper had found Perkins loading sand into a burlap bag in the yard of the Van Brunt Supply Company. Perkins stuck his shovel in the sand and said that, hell, he bore no grudge, hadn't since he had had time to think it over. A kid on a bicycle—well, Perkins drove a car himself. Things happen before you know it; things you can't do anything about. Bell had been decent enough about it—or his insurance company had.

As for the previous evening, Perkins had got home from work a little after five, had had dinner around six, and had stayed home until bedtime looking at TV. And they could ask his wife. His wife had been asked; had said he certainly had. Wives have been known to alibi for husbands. And it could not be denied that Perkins might, by a child, well be called a "thick" man.

But Malcolm Bell's body had not been found in Perkins's back yard. It had been found behind Philip Notson's garage. So Heimrich and Sergeant Forniss concentrated, most logically, on Bell himself and on Philip Notson.

Bell, on the last day of his life, had driven his wife to New York and put her on a plane for Palm Beach. He had driven back and had a drink at the Old Stone Inn, and told a friend he met there he was thinking about going around to see old Phil Notson and try to get things straightened out.

Half a dozen men had got off the 5:58 local-express at Van Brunt, and one of them might have been Notson, but they had not proved it by late afternoon.

Nobody had seen Notson on the 5:06, and since that was his regular train he probably would have been noticed and spoken to if he had been on it. Which did not prove much, since the most likely thing was that Notson had turned the garage flood-lights on at a little after nine to see who had come to the door and, when he found out, killed him. . . .

Nobody had showed up at the Blake house on Van Brunt Lane to say that they had had to stop to ask directions. Of course, the prospective droppers-in might merely have changed their minds . . . Ann's teacher said the poor little thing was a dear, but that she was a *most* imaginative child.

And—the eyes of cats do not shine red when light strikes them out of darkness. Heimrich had been sure of that, but all the same—since a policeman can never be too sure of any-thing—he had talked to an eye specialist he knew. "Nope," the ophthalmologist said, "not that I ever heard of. Oh—I suppose an albino cat's might. No pigment on the tapetum lucidum."

"The what?"

"Layer in the chorioid," the eye man said. "Back part of the eye. What reflects light. Good many mammals have it. We don't, more's the pity."

"Are there," Heimrich asked, "many albino cats?"

"One in a million, at a guess. I never saw one. Never met anybody who had seen one. They'd have pink eyes, of course. White cats with pink eyes."

A cat like that would be noticeable, Heimrich thought, and he asked around. Nobody had ever seen one. Not around there or anywhere else. So—Ann had not seen a red-eyed cat. A mil-lion to one she hadn't. And hence—not a man running, either, since the two things went together—went together in a child's imagination.

Heimrich turned his car off NY 11-F into Brickhouse Road. It was time to get to work on Philip Notson—to get really to work on him. It was dusk, then.

Heimrich switched the headlights on—and jammed his brakes on; and Sergeant Forniss, sitting beside him, put hands out to brace himself and said, "What the *hell?*"

"Look," Heimrich said, and they both looked—looked at two tiny lights by the road's edge; lights which glowed like coals in a fireplace, like the twin tail lights of a car. Red lights.

The little red lights went out. But then they were glowing from the top of a stone fence. They went out again, but by then Heimrich had the car off the road and they were out of it at a driveway.

There was enough light left to see a cat streak toward a house. A woman stood on the porch. The woman called, "*Boots! Here,* Boots. *Here—*" and then said to the arriving cat, "*You!* Again. *Again!*"

The woman was Mrs. Burnett—Mrs. Harry Burnett. Of course the cat belonged to her. "Come here, Boots," she said again, and Boots came to prove it.

"Oh," Heimrich said, and looked at Boots, who was certainly not a white cat with pink eyes; he was a cat with a black face and deep blue eyes and a black tail. "Oh," Heimrich said. "Siamese. We were looking for an albino cat." He could not remember that, as a policeman, he had ever made a sillier remark "A cat with red eyes," he added and felt sillier than ever, looking down at the blue-eyed cat.

"With red—" Mrs. Burnett said. "Oh—you mean with a light on them? Of course. They always are. Siamese eyes, I mean. Because Siamese are part albino, you know. Even if you'd never guess it to look at them."

It proved fortunate for Philip Notson—and for a little girl with greenish eyes and an imagination not quite, this time, as fervid as people were always saying—that Boots was a cat who led a somewhat circumscribed life; was a young female who, particularly at the moment, had her own idea about things, and hence was not let roam at large. But a cat who got out anyway, now and again, as she had this Saturday evening, but only for a few minutes.

The night before, however, Boots had got out at five thirty in the evening, Mrs. Burnett confided, and had been gone for an hour or more, and goodness knew where, and one could only hope.

Since two things were linked in the mind of a child, Heimrich and Forniss did not go on to the Notson house, but drove the other way—drove to The Flats and, with not much trouble found a "thick" man standing at the bar of the Three Oaks Tavern.

James Perkins did not seem surprised to see them, but then James Perkins was drunk now—mumbling drunk.

He mumbled a good deal about a so-and-so who thought he could get away with anything, and about bought-off so-and-sos who would let him. And about that so-and-so Bell, who knew better now, knew you couldn't cripple a kid and get off for a few measly dollars. Some drunken men talk a lot.

If Perkins talked enough, Heimrich thought, they might never have to ask a little girl if this was the man—the thick man—she had seen running.

But he would, he thought, some day make a point of telling a little girl that some cats do too have red eyes.

A WINTER'S TALE

A WINTER'S TALE

At a quarter after one on a Wednesday afternoon in mid-January, Florrie Watson parked her battered sedan and for a moment sat in it shivering, hugging a worn cloth coat around her. But there wasn't any use sitting there dreading it.

So she opened the car door, stepped out into the raging north-west wind, and ran—was half blown, for she was a little woman and not a young woman—to the kitchen door of the big drafty house on the hilltop. She had her key ready, turned it in the old-fashioned lock, tugged the door open, and let the wind slam it to behind her. It made noise enough, she thought, to wake the dead.

It was warm in the house and she took her coat off and hung it up before she did anything else. She found that she was listening for the old man to growl at her, to tell her angrily that she was late again. But there was no sound in the house, except the sound of the wind.

Florrie went into the living room, where she always started, and there was Aaron Stark, lying on the floor, wearing a nightshirt and a bathrobe over it. The low winter sun glared in through a window and he was lying on a rug in a patch of sunlight.

She called his name and then, again, more loudly, "Mr. Stark!" Then she made herself touch him. She had wasted breath calling him.

She had to go back into the bitter wind—it had been eight above when she left home and didn't seem to be getting any warmer—and drive half a mile to the nearest house because there was no telephone in the old Stark house. There had been one until about a year before, but Aaron Stark had quarreled with the telephone company with everybody—and jerked the instrument out of the wall, carried it out to the road, and thrown it down hard on the pavement. Which, he told Florrie, would teach them.

At the nearest neighbor's house Florrie Watson called the State Police.

The news that old Stark had died alone in his big barn of a house, four miles or so from Van Brunt Center, spread quickly. It was, people said, an awful thing to happen to anybody—to any old man, alone in a big drafty house. When they said "anybody" there was a just perceptible emphasis on "any"—as if the term were being stretched to include Aaron Stark.

That was the way people who lived in the town of Van Brunt felt about Aaron Stark, the old skinflint. People who knew Mary Phipps and her daughter, Joan, had even harder words for him. A man who won't help out his relatives when they are in bad trouble and he's got plenty is "no kind of a man." This was freely said by friends of Mary Phipps while Stark was alive, and when he was dead there were some who said, and many who thought, that now his money—of which it was generally agreed he had plenty—would go where it was needed, where it would do some good.

Captain M. L. Heimrich of the Bureau of Criminal Investigation, New York State Police, heard of Stark's death at around eight o'clock Wednesday evening. He went out of the biting cold—the forecast was for zero to ten below in Northern Westchester and Putnam counties, and Heimrich didn't doubt it for a minute—into the warm taproom of the Old Stone Inn at Van Brunt Center. He went, as any sensible man would on such a night, to the bar and Harold, the barman, pouring, said, "Hear about old Stark?"

Heimrich shook his head.

"Dead," Harold said. "Bad thing to happen to *any*body, dying alone that way." And he told Heimrich that the doc— "this new man, Smith; Doc Bender's in town at a meeting or something"—said that Stark had been dead twenty-four hours when he, as acting coroner, examined the body. At least twenty-four hours.

"Except," Harold said, detective to detective, "I'd figure it was longer, because that would make it yesterday afternoon, and what was he doing in a nightshirt in the afternoon?"

Heimrich said, "Hmmm" in appreciation of this reasoning. He took his drink over to the fireplace and stood with his back to the fire. "Probably woke up in the morning not feeling so good," Heimrich said, "and had a stroke. He must have been near eighty."

Actually, Heimrich was not too interested; he had known of Aaron Stark, but not known him. Surely Stark had died of natural causes or Heimrich would have heard by now, and death from natural cause, however sudden, was not a concern of Heimrich's. His concern was with homicide.

So Heimrich warmed his back, and then the bar telephone rang and Harold said into it, "Yep. Just come in."

Heimrich sighed. He went to the telephone and listened to an official voice. He said, "Okay. May as well start at the house," and finished his drink and put the glass down on the bar. Harold was looking at him. Harold might as well know—everybody would know soon enough. Things get around.

"Stark died of a fractured skull," Heimrich said, and went out of the taproom into the cold night and drove four miles to a hilltop and a lighted house. It was warm in the house. Little shivers of cold air roamed through it, but it was warm enough. Hot air poured up from an old-fashioned floor register. Heimrich could hear the furnace throbbing in the basement, straining against the cold.

The body had been removed hours before. Two state troopers were waiting for Heimrich. "Florrie Watson found him," one of them said. "She worked for him. Part time," and was asked if he knew where Florrie Watson lived. He did. She lived a mile and a half down the road.

"Go get her," Heimrich said and the trooper went, and Heimrich looked the house over.

It was a big house, an old house. Little money had been spent on it in many years, Heimrich thought. The wind whined in around loose-fitting windows, and scurried in under the kitchen door. It was surprising that it was as warm as it was, and Heimrich glanced at the thermostat and saw it was set for 80.

He went up a flight of stairs, opened the door, and a rush of cold air met him. The upper floor, evidently was not used; certainly was not heated. He went down the stairs, opened another door, and looked into darkness. The throbbing of the furnace was louder. He found Stark's bedroom, saw that the bed had been slept in but not made up.

Then the trooper brought in Florrie Watson—Mrs. Florence Watson, a little woman with red hands and straggling gray hair.

"I just thought he'd had a stroke or something," Florrie said. "I didn't dream..."

Heimrich was gentle. He was sorry he had had to ask her to come out on a night like this.

"This *weather*," she said. "Monday you wouldn't have thought it was January. Like April almost. And then like this."

People will talk about the weather under almost any circumstances, Heimrich thought; they will escape to the trivial, the safe.

"Yes," he said. "Where did you find him, Mrs. Watson?"

It had been about there, and she pointed. Near the center of the living room; near the center of an oval hooked rug. "In the sun," she had known at once that he was dead. She had called him, but known it was no good. Yes, the house had been locked when she came. The locks were not snap locks; you had to use the key. She came at one every afternoon, except Sunday, and worked until five, cleaning up and preparing dinner for Stark to warm up later when he wanted it. Breakfast and lunch he got for himself.

Heimrich said, "*Every* weekday? Then—"

"Not yesterday," she said. "I had one of my sick headaches. I started out and almost got here but I felt so sick—well, I just turned around and drove back home." She stopped suddenly. "If," she said, "if I'd come on I—I could have done something. That's what you mean?"

"Now, Mrs. Watson," Heimrich said. "It isn't likely you could have done anything for him. Just found him already dead, probably. He would have had to let in anyone who came? I mean, he always kept the doors locked?"

Always, so far as she knew. And she had the only extra key she knew about. Not that anybody ever came.

Somebody had come, Heimrich told her. That was clear enough.

"The trooper said he fractured his skull," Mrs. Watson said. "Couldn't he have fallen down and—?"

Heimrich shook his head. Stark had fallen, apparently, on the rug. If he had had a stroke, or merely fainted, he would almost certainly have slumped down, not fallen hard. And fallen on the padding of the rug. A fairly thick rug.

She didn't know. People never came. People didn't like him.

"You didn't like him?" Heimrich asked.

"Not to say liked," Florrie Watson said. "Put up with. It wasn't too far to come and I've got to work some place. Nag, nag, nag all the time, but I got so I didn't listen. "

"About the way you worked?"

"About everything. Wasting things, mostly. I don't waste. Not what you'd call waste. But what he called it—Well, he's dead now, the poor old thing."

Speak no evil, however tempted.

"Somebody came," Heimrich said. "Somebody killed him. Who would want to more than anyone else?"

She didn't know. But she hesitated, so Heimrich waited.

"Well," she finally said, "I don't like to say it. The girl said some mean things to him. Monday afternoon, that was. I don't know as I blame her, but—"

The girl was Joan Phipps, Aaron Stark's second cousin. She had come about four o'clock on Monday afternoon. She had quarreled with the old man and said that men like him ought to be dead.

"Not that I listened," Florrie Watson said. "More than I could help, anyway. But she raised her voice. And not that I blame her, mind you."

But that was Monday. Twenty-four hours from early Wednesday afternoon do not stretch back to Monday. However—

Joan Phipps had still been in the house on Monday when Florrie left at five o'clock. Talking loudly, "About money," Mrs. Watson said. "I can't deny I heard that much. Or that she and her mother need it—need it bad. You'd think even *he*—but there, he's dead now, the poor old soul."

Heimrich had known Mary Phipps, Aaron Stark's cousin and now presumably his heir—known her slightly, incuriously, as one knows a pleasant, hurried waitress. She had sometimes served Heimrich at the Old Stone Inn. A plump, quick, smiling woman in her late forties she was.

Driving from the drafty house toward The Flats, Heimrich recalled vaguely that she had quit the job sometime in the early fall. Something about her health. Yes, that was it.

He drove slowly on NY 11-F, which is Van Brunt Avenue through the Center, but only a number when it reaches the closely set, rundown little houses of The Flats. He kept his spotlight on rural mail boxes. At one marked Phipps he pulled to the side of the road.

The little house seemed to shake in the wind as he stood on the porch and knocked. After some seconds the door opened with a kind of violence and a tall, gangling girl looked at him. She said, "What do you want?"—with anger in her young voice. Heimrich told her who he was. The girl said, "How do I know?"—and Heimrich showed his badge.

It was not warm in the room she led him into—the room reeked of kerosene from a two-burner heater, but the room was not warm. The girl wore sweater over sweater, and a woolen skirt. She was, Heimrich guessed, about sixteen—tall and thin, with high shoulders, with cheekbones which made her face a triangle, with very wide eyes. And with red hair. The mouth was wide, too, its corners turned down—in a bitter mouth. Altogether, a sulky, angry girl. Quite possible with reason, Heimrich thought, and asked if he could see her mother.

"*No*, you can't," Joan Phipps said. "She's sick. You can leave her alone." She did not suggest that he sit down; she stood herself. "Leave us both alone," she said. "That's what everybody does." She was a lean young cat, snarling and spitting at the world.

"It's about your cousin," Heimrich said. "Your mother's cousin."

"All right," the girl said. "So he's dead. How do they tell the difference?"

Heimrich said, "Now, Miss Phipps."

"You want me to cry?" she said. "Go boo-hoo? Because he was always so good to us? Helped when it happened to Mother? When I had to quit school? When all he had to do—" She made an angry gesture with her thin hands.

"You told him this on Monday?" Heimrich said. "When you went there. When—"

"Say it," the girl said. "When I went begging. When—" Again she stopped, but this time, Heimrich thought, there was wariness in the wide, red-brown eyes.

"So what?" she said. "He didn't give me anything. He didn't die of giving me something. Not that it wouldn't have killed him."

"He died," Heimrich said, "of a fractured skull. From a blow of some sort. You went to ask help. He refused. You were angry. You shouted at him."

"Florrie Watson," Joan said. "Couldn't wait to blab, could she?"

But the voice was not the same. She was keyed up to my coming, Heimrich thought, keyed up to attack. Only she's a hurt child. Not what she wants to think she is. And—a frightened child?

"A fractured skull?" she said, and Heimrich merely nodded his head. "It couldn't be," she said. "All I did—you're trying to trick me."

"No," Heimrich said. "You hit him?"

"She can't live like this," the girl said. "Look—she can hardly move. When I have to go to work and leave her and—" She changed again. "You're like all of them," she said. "People like us are made to be pushed around. Just the way he—"

There could be no doubt why she stopped this time.

"He pushed you?" Heimrich said. "And—"

"Said things," she said. "All right, you've got what you came after. Things about—about Mother. And grabbed me and started to push and—I tell you, *I won't be pushed!* I won't—" But now she was near to tears.

"You hit him?" Heimrich said. "With what?"

"This," she said, and shook her closed right fist. Two knuckles of the fist were still reddened, bruised.

"He fell?"

"Fell? Of course not. He said—he called me a name and started toward me again—and I ran. And he locked the door after me. I heard it. So he was all right and—" Once more she stopped. "He was all right?" she said, and questioned like a child.

"It doesn't always take much," Heimrich said. "How was he dressed, Miss Phipps?"

She repeated vaguely, "Dressed?" and then she said that Stark had worn ordinary things—gray trousers and a sweater, she thought.

"Joan?" a shaking voice called from another room—from, Heimrich suspected, the only other room. "Is somebody there?"

The girl looked at Heimrich. And Heimrich shook his head, turned to the door, and went out of the little house.

He would have to come back, of course—first check with the doctor and then come back—when he had verified formally what he knew to be true: that a relatively light blow may fracture a thin skull; that the victim may not lose consciousness for hours and then go into a coma and die; that a man hurt that way might very well lock a door and even undress and go to bed and wake up later and start a search for help. And die hours after the blow. Of—what was it?—a subdural hemorrhage in the brain. That was it. So an angry girl, striking back like a child, might have killed the old man.

The radio in Heimrich's car squawked at him. He was to telephone Dr. Robert Bender, county coroner, at his first opportunity. Heimrich telephoned from the inn. He listened. He said, "What?" in a tone of incredulity. Then, "Come again, Doctor."

"A quite easy mistake to make," Dr. Bender said. "Even a much more experienced man might have been misled during a preliminary examination. With further examination, Dr. Smith himself would—er—have realized that the fracture was postmortem. I don't doubt that. I—"

"All right," Heimrich said. "I've no doubt Dr. Smith is a very able man. Ice in the skull expands and separates skull sutures and—"

"The coronal suture in this case," Dr. Bender said. "Very similar to an ante-mortem fracture on first—"

"All right, Doctor," Heimrich said. "What you're telling me now is that old Stark *froze* to death. And that his brain turned to ice, expanded, and broke his skull? And that if he was hit earlier, say, that had nothing to do with his death?"

"That's it," Dr. Bender said. "Got to you with it as fast as I could."

Heimrich thanked him for that much and put the telephone back in its cradle. He looked hard at it as if it were to blame.

It had been so simple—an angry child, a blow, an old man's thin skull. And now—Now he had a man freezing to death in a warm house—a house with a thermostat set at 80°. Because nobody would have gone out of a house in nightshirt and bathrobe with the bottom falling out of the thermometer and stayed outside long enough to freeze—and then—then what? Walked back in again and lain down on the living-room rug?

A problem for a detective—a nagging problem. Nagging? Why—?

Oh, Heimrich thought, and made two telephone calls. Power had not been off Monday night in the area. The five hundred and fifty-gallon oil tank in the basement of Aaron Stark's house had been filled only a week before. So.

Heimrich went back into the cold night and drove away. He drove past Stark's big, drafty house and a mile and a half on down the road. Florrie Watson was still up—it was as if she had been waiting. She looked up at him with fear, without surprise.

"Mrs. Watson," Heimrich said, and went into the very warm—the almost stifling—living room of her little house. "Mrs. Watson, Mr. Stark froze to death. You knew that, didn't you?"

She pushed at straggling gray hair and looked quickly away, and then nodded her head.

"You did go to the house yesterday." Heimrich said. "And turned the furnace on again, and the thermostat up high. When you found him dead. Thinking—thinking nobody'd ever know you'd turned the furnace *off* the day before?"

"He was always nagging," the little woman said in a voice from far away. "How was I to know it would get so cold?"

The radio had carried the forecast, the warning of a severe cold wave. It had been in all the newspapers. Which didn't matter too much.

"He always kept the place like a morgue," she said in the same distant voice. "Wouldn't let me turn the thermostat up—wasted oil, he said. Always nagging about it. I said, 'You want me to get pneumonia?' and—" Her voice died away. Heimrich waited.

"Put the mop and things back in the basement before I left Monday," she went on. "And there was the switch—the furnace switch—and I thought, I'll show him. I'll save his oil for him." Again she stopped. But then she put her hands up to her flat chest and began to back away from Heimrich.

"*I didn't know!*" she said, and her voice was almost a scream. "I didn't mean it to happen. *All I wanted was to teach him a lesson!*"

Drafty old houses on hilltop—such houses cool quickly when the wind rages and the temperature drops hard. Old men might wake up shivering in such houses, get out of bed to find out what had gone wrong, get up too suddenly into bitter cold. Faint from shock, perhaps? They would never know, precisely. That also didn't matter too much.

Mrs. Watson had taught her lesson, if that was really all she had had in mind. Others would have to decide about that.

"You'd better come along with me, Mrs. Watson," Heimrich said kindly. "Wrap up warm. It's cold outside."

THE ACCUSING SMOKE

THE ACCUSING SMOKE

It would do no good to go out of the house and stand at the head of the driveway and look down it. That wouldn't make him come any sooner. It would be foolish to do that, as it was foolish to be so worried.

One does not drive more than sixty miles into New York to take one's wares to market, drive back again, and do it all on schedule. Only—he had been quite certain he would be back long before dark, and it was beginning to grow dark.

Sally Brent went out of the house in the hills near Brewster— the house which was almost all painter's studio, with a small bedroom off a balcony and a gas plate behind a curtain. She walked a little way down the rough driveway, which was paved from the road to the big house, but not after it half circled the big house and climbed on to the studio.

She listened and did not hear the car; she gazed anxiously into the semi-darkness and did not see a car's lights. It was getting cooler, Sally Brent thought, and the wind's rising—oh, I wish he'd come home! And somebody's burning leaves, which is a danger with everything outdoors so dry.

She sniffed again. Not the smoke scent of leaves burning. Of course not—it was wood smoke in the late October air. And with the wind blowing as it was, wood smoke from the big house—from Uncle Roger's house.

Only—Uncle Roger wasn't there. Or wasn't supposed to be. The house was closed, or was supposed to be. Closed since August when Uncle Roger had gone to Europe. If he had come back this Friday afternoon, surely he would have let them know.

They were supposed to keep an eye on things—that was a way of paying rent for the studio house. About the only way we have, Sally thought, without bitterness—the only way until "They" find out how good an artist Jim really is.

She went on down the rough, curving drive—a slight girl of twenty-two, in country slacks and simple sweater. When she had gone far enough to glimpse the big house, there was still light enough to see that smoke was coming from the central chimney, blowing toward her.

There were no lights on in the big house. She hurried a little, for no special reason. She knocked on the living-room door and, unanswered, pushed at it and it opened. She called, "Uncle Roger?" before the smoke in the room began to choke her.

The fireplace damper again, she thought. Stuck and— She tried to call again, and made only a coughing sound. She stepped back out of the living room and filled her lungs with fresher air, then crouched low and ran into the room.

Get the windows open, get air in! Her eyes streamed; she held her breath, ran across the room to the windows, pulled two open, leaned out through one, and breathed again. Air flowed in through the open windows and after a moment she turned back into the room, groped her way across it, and found a light switch.

He lay on the wide, polished floorboards near the fireplace from which smoke was still billowing. She called again, knew it was no use, and looked at the floor around him; then, because of what she saw, she looked at her own feet. She was wearing gray loafers. She had walked through blood in them. Now she ran in them—back to the studio, away from death . . .

Age; middle sixties. A big man, who had almost certainly been still a strong man. Probably knocked unconscious by the first blow from the heavy poker. Dead not much more than an hour, the medical examiner thought. Quite probably, the first blow had been enough, but there had been more—a good many more.

"All right," Captain M. L. Heimrich, New York State Police, said, "You can take him along."

They took the body of Roger Handley along.

Heimrich glanced around the big room. Costly for a summer place, Heimrich thought. There was a faint, by no means unpleasant, odor of wood smoke in the room. Heimrich, circling the blood which was drying now, went to the fireplace and looked down at it. The fire had gone out, or nearly. Probably never had quite taken hold; the big logs were only a little charred.

Heimrich crouched and then looked up the chimney. He reached back and said, "Got a flashlight, Charlie?" and when Sergeant Charles Forniss provided one, the Captain sent the beam up the chimney. Damper three-quarters closed. No wonder there had been smoke, no wonder the fire had not taken hold. Heimrich tried the lever and when nothing happened, he tugged hard. "Stuck," he said and started to stand up and stopped, sitting on his heels.

Fallen on either side of the fire-dogs were the ends of the lightweight wood which had been used as kindling, and had burned enough, draft or no draft. The ends of sticks, some as big around as a wrist—a small wrist. And—a hairy wrist. Not what I'd pick to use as kindling, Heimrich thought, and stood up—a solid man of a little more than average height, with a solid face.

"Let's go talk to the niece," Heimrich said. "This Mrs. Brent who found him—and called us." Forniss, who was a little taller than Heimrich, and even more solid, raised his eyebrows. "Not unless she's an Amazon, Charley," Heimrich said. "Find anything that helps?"

"Nope," Forniss said. "No forced entry. Handle of the poker wiped clean. Tracks part way to the window—but you saw that. Walked through blood on her way. You'd think she'd have noticed."

"The room was still pretty smoky when the boys got here," Heimrich said. "Even with a cross draft. You don't see much in smoke. Anything else?"

Forniss shrugged. He said there was nothing that meant much so far as he could see. However— In the waste-basket, a torn up envelope, addressed to Roger Handley, RFD 1, Brewster, New York. Woman's handwriting; postmark, White Plains, N.Y., August 11. No return address. On a table, a copy of the New York *Herald-Tribune,* dated August 12. Came through the mail. Forniss raised his eyebrows again.

"Let's go up to this studio," Heimrich said. "See if the lady's an Amazon."

She was not that; she was anything but that—a slender girl, not tall; a girl with the fragility of the small-boned. The light-boned can be stronger than they look, but not that much stronger—not strong enough to crush a man's skull with the first blow of a poker.

Sally Brent was also beautiful. Heimrich could not recall more than one or two times before when he had seen a woman to whom that absolute could be applied. Her eyes now, as she stood in the shelter of her husband's arm, were wide with shock. Or, conceivably, with fear. There was no easy way of telling which.

The man who seemed to protect her would have made two of her by weight—a big man, with the slightly sloping shoulders of an athlete. After the first moments of making common cause—but why that?—in the doorway, James and Sally Brent drew back from the doorway and Brent said, "We've been waiting for you."

The room was long; the far wall was sloping glass. There was an easel at that end, with a covered canvas on it. Along both side walls other canvases were stacked. The third of the room nearest the door was furnished and lighted as a living room. There was nothing here that had cost much—not like the big house. There were many pictures on the walls—oils, sketches.

James Brent had often sought to catch his wife's beauty and hold it quiet on canvas.

"A bad thing to walk in on," Heimrich said. "You feel up to talking about it, Mrs. Brent?"

For a second she only looked at him from wide, dark eyes. Then she nodded her head slowly, each slow motion distinct, and said in a soft voice, "Of course." She told him of the scent of wood smoke in the evening air, of going to the big house, of the smoke there, of what she saw when the light was on. She looked down at her feet then, and there was a tremor in her slender body. But she had changed her shoes; there was no blood on these.

"You didn't think your uncle would be there?" Heimrich said.

James Brent answered that. They had known he was about due back from Europe, but not that he was back. Certainly they had not expected him up. He seldom came to the country this late in the fall.

"Anyway," Brent said, "he usually called us first. To get fires started, do the chores—we do that sort of thing for this. It must have been a spur-of-the-moment idea for him."

Brent sat beside his wife on a sofa and Heimrich sat facing them. Forniss was a statue by the door. Brent gestured to indicate "this"—that "this" was the studio. He wore a short-sleeved polo shirt. There was an angry red rash on both his wrists. Brent stopped in the gesture and looked at his wrists, because Heimrich was looking at them.

"Poison ivy," James Brent said, and gazed at Heimrich as if the detective had asked a question the purpose of which was obscure. "Been cleaning up around the place. Mostly for exercise. Ivy was choking some of the young trees. Thought I was covered up but—"

"There was a good deal of ivy in the brushwood that Mr. Handley used to start the fire," Heimrich remarked.

Brent looked puzzled. Sally Brent looked as if she were not listening, as if she were looking at something far away.

"I made a brush pile," Brent said. "Too dry outside to burn it now. I suppose he took some off the pile. He's—he was—immune to the stuff. Like Sally is. Like I'm not." He looked again at his wrists. The blisters had started.

"Captain," Sally said in the soft voice, and now she looked directly at Heimrich, not at something infinitely far away. "Wasn't it—just somebody who broke in? A tramp? A burglar? And Uncle Roger came in and—" She paused. "He usually carried quite a lot of money," she said.

"Perhaps," Heimrich said. "But there was more than two hundred dollars in his wallet, Mrs. Brent. Untouched. And breaking into a house can be a noisy business. You didn't hear anything?"

She had not; not anything. Not, specifically, the sound of a car going to or leaving the big house. But she would not have—there was a hill between. In the studio she wouldn't have heard any ordinary or small noises.

"How did you happen to go out?" Heimrich said. "So that you smelled the smoke?" The question was innocent enough, or nearly so. But it brought fear—surely fear this time—into the wide, dark eyes.

"Just—" she said. "No reason—to see if—I heard the wind coming up and—"

Brent reached out. He took both her slender hands in one of his. He said, "Wait. Wait, Sally." Her eyes turned away.

"I was late," Brent said. "I'd driven into town to take some stuff to my agent. Expected to get back a good deal earlier than I did. She'd gone out to see if I was coming. Got—well, anxious, I guess. And now she's afraid you'll—get ideas." He looked at Heimrich, and his look challenged the detective.

"May as well get it straight," Brent went on. "On the record. Handley had a lot of money. In the ordinary course Sally will get it. And—we can use it." He gestured again around the sparsely furnished room. "And—I wasn't late in getting home because I stopped on the way. At the big house. For—any purpose."

Questions answered before questions asked. Which didn't really mean anything.

"Why were you late?" Heimrich said.

"Car conked out. This side of Golden's Bridge. Just stopped. Walked a mile or so to a house, but nobody was there. Walked back and decided to give it another try. And—it started."

Now they both looked at Heimrich—and their eyes waited.

"Dirt in the carburetor probably," Heimrich said. "Happens that way sometimes."

(And when it does there is no need to call a repair man, who would remember being called . . . or, of course, deny being called.)

The wariness, the fear, did not go out of the girl's wide eyes. Was she, Heimrich wondered, afraid only of what the police might think? Or—of what she thought herself?

James Brent still held his wife's slender hands. It was impossible to see whether they still trembled.

"Your uncle," Heimrich said. "He was—what, Mrs. Brent? Your father's brother?" She nodded. "There are other relatives?"

She shook her head. "Not since Aunt Mary died," she said. "His sister. Not since that—that other awful thing."

She turned then and stared at her husband—stared up at him. Seated, Brent still was tall.

"Mary Parkins," Brent said. "Mrs. Clement Parkins?"

The inflection meant, or seemed to mean, that the name should be familiar to Heimrich. It wasn't. Heimrich shook his head to show it wasn't.—

"Early last month," Brent explained. "She fell from the balcony of their apartment in White Plains. Nobody knows how. There was a rail. You'd have thought—" He shrugged. "Got dizzy," he said.

"That was the only guess anybody made. Only half an hour earlier she was fine. I was driving through White Plains that

day and stopped to say hello and she gave me a drink and—"
Again he shrugged. "It's all in the records," he said. "Nothing
to do with this."

He had freed Sally's hands as he spoke. Now, abruptly, she
lifted her hands and hid her face in them.

"Nothing to do with this," James Brent said again, and his
voice was louder. "Not a damn thing."

Which, Heimrich thought, was a foolish thing for him to
say since there had been two who might have inherited Roger
Handley's money—and now there was only one. And now
Roger Handley was also dead. And as Brent said, there would
be records to show Brent had been with Mary Parkins just
before she died.

"Now, Mr. Brent," Heimrich began, but a car door slammed
outside and he stopped. There was a hurried knocking at
the door and Forniss opened it. The man who came in, who
brushed past Forniss, was broad—a heavy man. He stopped
and looked around, his wide face set. He shook his head, as if
bewildered.

"Hello, Uncle Clem," Sally Brent said. "Uncle Roger's been—
he's been killed."

"They told me that," the heavy man said. He spoke in a
heavy voice. "Stopped down at the house and they told me
that. It's—it's hard to believe. That anybody—" He stopped,
turned to Heimrich, and Heimrich identified himself.

"Parkins," the heavy man said. "Clement Parkins. Rog called
me this afternoon and said to come up. I get here and—" He
spread his hands. "Who did it? Who'd do a thing like that to
Rog?"

"I don't know yet," Heimrich said. "You say he called you?"
Asked you to come up? Why, Mr. Parkins?"

"Something about—" Parkins stopped abruptly and looked
at Sally Brent on the sofa. She looked back at him steadily. (Too
steadily?) "I'd rather—" He seemed to consider.

"All right," he said. "I'm—I was—his lawyer. As well as his brother-in-law. You know about that? About my wife and—"

"Yes," Heimrich said. "He wanted you to come up as his lawyer? Why?"

Again Parkins seemed to consider.

"Well," he hesitated, "about his will. He—he planned to change it. With Mary—" He swallowed as if the name choked him. "With Mary dead," he said. "She and Sally inherited or—" Once more he stopped; once more he looked at Sally Brent, fragile and still on the sofa. "Or the survivor," Parkins finished.

It did not need clearer saying, and Parkins's face said as much to Heimrich. "Do I have to spell it out? With her here?" With one heir dead, the other inherited. If that was the way Handley wanted it, he would not have needed to change his will.

"I admit I don't know what he planned," Parkins said, making that scrupulously clear . . .

"It's pretty open and shut," Forniss said, as they drove away half an hour later—drove from the studio, past the big house; drove away from a fragile and beautiful girl with fear living in her eyes, and a painter with the muscles of an athlete, his wrists inflamed by the poison of *Toxicodendron radicans,* a vine which climbs over walls and up trees on hairy stems.

Heimrich did not answer at once. Forniss took his eyes from the road long enough to look at Heimrich.

"In twenty-four hours it ought to be," Heimrich said. "Maybe a little longer."

There were odds and ends to check. Handley had filed a change of address at the Brewster post office, directing that all his mail be sent to his New York apartment. Yes, there had—and how had Heimrich guessed?—been a substitute carrier on Route One on August 12. He might have slipped up.

The White Plains police hadn't liked the manner of Mary Parkins's death—hadn't liked it at all. The guard rail was high enough. But they had not been able to prove that James Brent had not left the Parkins apartment half an hour before Mary Parkins fell, as he claimed he had—or that Clement Parkins had been there at all, as he claimed he hadn't.

Yes, the handwriting on the envelope addressed to Roger Handley in Brewster was almost certainly that of Mary Parkins. Yes, her life had been rather heavily insured, with double indemnity in, case of accidental death . . .

At eight o'clock Saturday evening the trooper who had stopped by the studio, on a pretext, called Heimrich at the Hawthorne barracks to say that it was still just on the wrists. So Heimrich drove the few miles to White Plains and I found that Clement Parkins was J not in his apartment, but in White Plains Hospital, which did not surprise Heimrich at all.

"No," the resident doctor at the hospital said, "you can't, Captain. He's under pretty deep sedation. He's really got it bad. All over. He'll live but—man, he must have waded in it."

"Or," Heimrich said, "got a lot of it in smoke. In a room full of smoke, say."

The doctor agreed: a lot of it in smoke would explain it.

Spadework, remained, of course, before they could charge Clement Parkins with the willful murder of Roger Handley. Some of it might take time, and not be easy. How, for example, prove that Mary Parkins, with cause to fear her husband—an earlier attempt that had failed?—had written her fears to her brother? The letter was certainly ashes now—the tardy letter, read long after it could do her any good because a substitute mail carrier had, understandably enough, slipped up. That it had been read was obvious enough and that Handley had summoned his brother-in-law to explain and that Parkins—with no explanation available and with the knowledge that a murder investigation is never closed—had killed again instead.

A good deal to be dug into, to be proved. But not that Parkins had been in the room when the smoke filled it—and therefore when Handley died in it. That had proved itself—very uncomfortably for Clement Parkins who would, however, face more extreme discomforts.

Hadn't the man known, Heimrich wondered, driving north, that his brother-in-law had started a smoky fire with poison ivy brush as kindling? Or hadn't he known that the irritant poison of *Toxicodendron radicans* rides in the smoke of its burning, and is virulent there?

Heimrich drove on toward Brewster with a cheerful duty to discharge. As a policeman he must, perforce, often frighten. It is pleasant when he can, with a few words, erase fright from a beautiful girl's dark eyes.

FLAIR FOR MURDER

FLAIR FOR MURDER

The dog was constantly bringing things home. This time the thing was a green felt hat with a small, meaningless feather sticking up from its band—a long-worn hat. The dog, whose name was Leonard, carried it over the stone fence from the Blaine place and brought it to Martin Olds, who stopped the power mower just in time. Leonard, not an especially brave dog—almost all cats bullied him—was unawed by power mowers, being confident that they stopped whenever he looked at them.

"Now what?" Martin Olds asked the dog, in that tone of exasperated fondness which was the only tone to adopt with Leonard. The dog opened a large and dripping mouth in a pleased grin, having received the expected praise. Olds reached down for the hat and Leonard became roguish.

"No," Olds said firmly, and held onto the hat.

It was John Adams' hat—the only hat, so far as Martin Olds knew that Old John had ever had. When Martin was a boy, Old John had worn that hat, and twenty years ago he had worn the same hat. Across the wall between the Olds place and the Blaine place, Martin, a boy of thirteen, would say, "Good morning, Mr. Adams," and Adams would say, " 'Lo, sonny," and take off the feathered hat, mop his forehead, and put the hat on again.

Adams, the Blaine caretaker, had still been wearing the hat two days ago when Martin met him in North Wellwood Center—met him for the first time in three years. Adams had taken his hat off in the old way, mopped his forehead with a clean white handkerchief, and said, " 'Lo, Mr. Olds. Back to stay?"

Martin had said he was afraid not, and had started to ask, "How's Miss Blaine?" But he'd stopped himself partly because Nancy wasn't "Miss Blaine" any longer—hadn't been for almost the same three years. And partly for other reasons.

It was hard to imagine John Adams' hat without Old John under it; but there it was now, with only wisps of grass under it. Martin turned the hat around in strong brown hands—the sun burns hands brown in South America, if one is out in it enough. And if a man is second man on a dam construction job, he is out in it enough.

The hat was dirty, which was understandable. But—earth was ground into it. The hat looked as if Leonard had buried it and then dug it up again. I should, Martin Olds thought, let Liz go over and explain. He's her dog. But Martin's sister was at a garden club meeting, which was to be expected, and Old John would surely be missing his hat.

So Martin took long strides to the stone fence, stepped to its top and then down, and was on a path between neat rows of vegetables, well along for late May. Old John's vegetables were always well along, always had been. Beyond rows of young beans there was a rectangle where the raked earth was brown and in which nothing grew—and in the middle of which was the kind of hole a dog digs when he's after something.

Martin Olds walked between rows of beans and looked into the hole. Then he swore sharply and was down on his knees, pawing the earth with his hands. He did not have to paw long—just long enough to make sure there was a foot still in the shoe that a digging dog had uncovered.

Martin Olds ran back, although he knew running would not help. It was a little before five when he reached a telephone in his sister's house, which was nearer than the Blaine house. The New York State Police logged his call in at exactly 4:53 . . .

Charles liked her to be arranged, crisp and clean and smiling, making a pretty picture of a young wife awaiting the return of her husband from his city labors. Nancy Compton arranged herself, at a little after five that Thursday afternoon, and knowing that she always so prepared herself for the advent of Charles, felt something almost like guilt—as if, in doing just what Charles wanted, she were at the same time subtly ridiculing her own husband. Which was, she told herself, utterly absurd. I love him, she told herself—and tried not to be conscious that she told herself this with a kind of determination. Of course I want things the way he wants them—to be the pretty picture of a waiting wife. And of course it isn't true that he's more interested in the picture than—

She stretched her slender body, in its lovely dress, on a chaise on the terrace, where he would see her as he drove onto the turnaround. Leaf shadows moved across her slim brown legs. A pretty picture of a waiting girl, and a *true* picture. I haven't any doubts, she told herself—no *real* doubts. It's just that I'm a little upset about things in general—starting, most prosaically, with this slight, persistent cold. Probably that's really the most important thing. I'm a little under par physically and so—

Certainly there was no reason to be disturbed because old John Adams hadn't been near the house for two days. There was nothing she could tell him about taking care of the big place. He had been taking care of it, with no advice from anybody, for a quarter of a century. "You're the best judge of that, John," her father had always told John Adams, and neither of them had had any doubt that what Arthur Blaine said was true. Sometimes Old John hadn't come near the house for days— had been a faraway, stocky figure, with rake or mower, or a squatting figure setting out plants, or a man distantly busy in his potting shed. It was true that in recent months, since a little after Arthur Blaine died, Old John had come to the house more frequently—daily, sometimes several times a day—and now and then on what Nancy suspected to be pretexts.

This touched her. He still thought of her as a child, a lonely child, with her father dead and a commuting husband. She sometimes, secretly, wished Charles were not quite so resolute about keeping on with his city job. The job wasn't really good enough for him, and with all her father had left them—left her, but it was the same thing, of course—what Charles earned wasn't really needed. But she could never tell him that—not a man like Charles Compton, who had a picture of himself as he had one of her.

Yes, it was touching. For what Old John had been doing was to keep an eye on a child. That he had now, suddenly and for forty-eight hours, stopped doing it was—well, puzzling. Earlier that day, puzzlement had led her to telephone his house, at the far end of the big estate, out of sight from the main house. There had been no answer, but that meant nothing. Good care-takers have little time to be inside houses in the month of May.

And there was—hardly an admissible contribution to her vague uneasiness about the shape of things in general—the fact that Martin Olds was "home" again. Not that the house next door was any longer his home. It was a place in which he visited his maiden sister, briefly, before going off again to some other end of the earth. And that he was there meant nothing to her. Except, since he had made no effort to see her, or even to call her, that he had not forgiven her for preferring Charles. It was better that way—better in all respects. Except there was no reason they shouldn't be friends again. This way made it seem more important than it ever really was.

It was 5:30, or about that, when she first heard, then saw, the familiar car coming up the drive. So Charles had caught the early train, as he had hoped to do. She felt instant relief. His presence—his solid, familiar presence, his assured presence—would brush these foolish cobwebs from her mind.

Charles got out of the car—a solid man in his middle thir-ties, a man with a pleasant, open face—and after she had given him a moment to see the picture he so liked, Nancy put a slim brown hand on each metal arm of the chaise and pulled herself up.

There was a sudden sharp pain across the fingers of her right hand. She looked at the hand in surprise. There was a gash across two fingers and a good deal of blood. She said, "Oh!" and shook the bleeding hand.

What a way to spoil things! And how on earth? A hundred times she had used her hands to pull herself out of the chaise and there had been no jagged metal—

"Nancy!" Charles said in quick alarm, coming to her. "Child!" he said. "How—" He stopped with that.

"Clumsy," she said. "I'm always so—"

He interrupted. He said, rather sharply, "Nonsense, Nancy," and took her injured hand in both of his. "We'll have to get something on that," he told her. He took a handkerchief from the breast pocket of his jacket and wrapped it around Nancy's hand. "I'll get the merthiolate," he said, and then looked resentfully at the chaise. "Crime the way they throw these things together nowadays," he muttered, and went into the house.

Trust me to spoil the picture, Nancy thought, and sat down on the edge of the chaise to wait. There was blood—her blood—on the underside of the metal arm of the chaise. Sharp edge, obviously. Funny she had never—

John Adams had been a broad-shouldered, weathered man in his early—and obviously vigorous—seventies. He had had broad hard hands. He had been shot once, accurately, near the heart and had been buried in a new asparagus bed. A hole had been dug, planted roots lifted out, the body placed under them, the roots put back, and the bed raked smooth. That much was evident to Captain M. L. Heimrich, New York State Police, whose professional concern was with homicide.

An ingenious place to dispose of the body, Heimrich thought, looking down at it. New digging explained, which was always something of a problem when they buried. And, even more important, in a place where the soil would not again be disturbed for years since, once planted, asparagus is left to its own devices for a decade or so. It was pure chance the dog had dug there. Unless—

Heimrich reached down and lifted a handful of soil. He sniffed. Bone meal. Not pure chance, after all. The dog had, in a sense, been invited.

"Why would anybody want to kill Old John?" Martin Olds asked, standing tall beside Heimrich. "He was a swell old guy. Everybody around here liked him."

So far as Heimrich had discovered from the briefing by a trooper who knew the area well, everybody had liked John Adams, and called him "Old John." Except, clearly, at least one person—a person with a gun. A .38 from the looks of things, and they would know definitely, because the bullet was still in Adams' thick body. Which was the reason a murderer had sought permanent burial. Slugs from rifled firearms are communicative.

Thirty years as caretaker of the Blaine estate, Adams had been an institution in North Wellwood, as Arthur Blaine him-self had been. One of the few big-estate owners hereabouts who hadn't broken up his acreage—Blaine didn't have to. What he had left his daughter when he died was anybody's guess—any high guesser's. And Charles Compton, who had married Nancy Blaine two years before her father died, had come into a good thing.

Not that anybody grudged it to him—a substantial citizen, Charles Compton was, even if he was not a local, even if he was a city man. Some men whose wives had inherited as much as Nancy had would have knocked off work. Not Charles Compton. Even those who had expected her to marry Martin Olds, and were still a little surprised that she hadn't—the two had more or less grown up together—agreed that Compton was an all-right guy.

All of which, Heimrich thought, was rather far from the immediate problem. He said, "Well, thanks, Mr. Olds"—in a tone which dismissed—and "All right, Ted," to the trooper who knew his way around the area. He and the trooper walked through the vegetable garden, past an old asparagus bed—petering out, it was, which accounted for the new one—and along a path, up a hill and down on the other side, to the cottage in which John Adams had lived alone—a neat, well-kept place. And not, they decided quickly, the place in which Adams had died. There were no signs of that, and there would have been.

Adams' work shed—his tool shed, potting shed—was a hundred yards or so from his cottage. It was there he had been killed: that was evident at once from bloodstains on the rough wood flooring. Somebody, Heimrich thought, had tried to scour the stain off the wood and when that failed, the murderer had dirtied it with soil. It still showed.

At one end of the shed there were wooden shelves and one cupboard with a door and a padlock—a broken padlock. So—it was as simple as that: a thief come upon, a thief turned killer on the instant. As routine as that. What, Heimrich wondered mildly, had the thief expected to find in a wooden cupboard in a tool shed? A miser's hidden gold? And why the tool shed, rather than the cottage which had not, Heimrich was certain, been ransacked?

Heimrich shrugged. There is no real accounting for the actions of minor criminals. He opened the cupboard.

Insecticides. Fungicides. In cans and boxes, a good many of them marked POISON. So the padlock was accounted for. Keep poisons locked away, especially from curious children who roam far in the country and are seldom above trespassing.

Heimrich kept cataloguing the shelves. Cut worm bait—active ingredient, arsenic. Rat poison—arsenic again, or thallium, or strychnine. Bichloride of mercury—Old John had been having trouble with cabbage root maggots ... Enough poison here to kill hundreds. But apparently poison had not been what the thief was after, since he had left so much behind.

Heimrich closed the cupboard. He looked around the shed, his countryman's mind admiring its order. Dry sprayers and wet sprayers arranged in a corner, an arsenal against insects and the ills that plants are heir to. One large, squat bottle half filled with a milky liquid. Heimrich did not at once identify the liquid. He went to the sprayer, picked it up, and shook it. It foamed soapily. Heimrich unscrewed the top, smelled the liquid, screwed the top back on again. It was a day for using his nose. Nicotine in a laundry soap solution. A good thing for tomato aphids. Funny, though, he hadn't seen—

He went back to the cupboard and looked again, this time with a special purpose. There was no small and deadly bottle of nicotine solution. Used up in making this last batch? Likely enough. Still—

"Let's go up to the big house, Ted," Heimrich said. "Tell them about Mr. Adams."

I'm spoiling everything, Nancy Compton thought, and felt a kind of shamed embarrassment. The martini, served in a chilled glass from a beaded silver shaker, had no flavor. The stubborn cold had evidently reached that stage—her sense of smell dimmed, hence her sense of taste diminished.

But it was more than that—although she had drunk less than half her drink, she felt a vague dizziness, a hint of nausea. So the picture was spoiled again—the ritual of terrace cocktails, which Charles so prized, was marred, ruined.

And her hand hurt—it hurt more than it should, hurt with a burning pain under the plastic bandages Charles had wrapped around her cut fingers, wrapped so tenderly after applying the merthiolate. Which was certainly strange, because merthiolate stings only briefly, does not really burn.

"You all right?" Charles had changed from city clothes, as ritual provided, and now his tone was anxious. "You look—"

He stopped, because a car had come up the drive and halted on the turnaround. Two men got out. One was tall and solid and in slacks and jacket; the other was a New York State Trooper in uniform. Charles Compton stood up slowly and waited for the two men to cross to the terrace.

"State Police," the man in civilian clothes said. "Afraid I've got some bad news for you. John Adams has been killed. Found his body buried in—"

Compton was a pleasant-looking man, Heimrich thought, as he told the rest. His wife was very pretty—brown-haired and blue-eyed and very pretty. She seemed to stare strangely, though. Heimrich moved closer. Pupils dilated.

Heimrich watched the girl as he told them. She said, "Not John! Not—" and started to stand up, swayed and staggered.

All three started toward her, but Heimrich was the nearest and caught her as she fell. He lifted her to the chaise and then, bending over her, caught up her bandaged right hand and held it to his nose. His day for using his nose, certainly.

"Ted!" Heimrich said, his usually soft voice sharp. "Call—no, drive Mrs. Compton to the hospital. Get her there fast!"

"Hospital?" Charles Compton said. "She's—"

"*Fast*, Ted," Heimrich told the trooper again, and as if Compton were not there. "And get another cruiser here and—"

"I'll go with them," Compton said, and the words ran over each other. "She can't be—Nancy!"

But Nancy Compton, being carried to the police car, did not hear him. Compton moved then—moved, obviously, toward the garage, toward his own car.

"No," Heimrich said, and stood in front of him. "A couple of questions first, Mr. Compton. Adams was shot. I'm looking for the gun—a thirty-eight, I'd guess. So if you don't mind—"

It was really foolish to try to run, but some men are foolish. And it had been sprung on Charles Compton so suddenly. John Adams was buried—safely buried for as long as the asparagus grew in its new bed.

Stopped from running—Heimrich produced a gun as deter-
rent—Compton's face showed fear. It also showed a kind of
disbelief.

"Bone meal," Heimrich told him. "When you plant asparagus,
Mr. Compton, you plant it deep. The old-timers do, anyway—and
with enough fertilizer to last for years. Bone meal, among other
things. And bone meal—ground bone—smells like a bone to a
dog. And dogs, Mr. Compton, dig for bones. Where's *your* gun,
Mr. Compton?"

They found Compton's gun—the right gun for the police,
therefore the wrong one for Compton. Heimrich told Martin
Olds about it after Compton had been taken away.

This was at a little before midnight, and the two waited at the
North Wellwood Hospital—waited to be told. Heimrich spoke
also about the dog, explained that dogs often dig where bone
meal has been freely used. He said, "A countryman would
have known better. Picked a better place—where there was no
bone meal to invite a dog."

Olds made a quick gesture, dismissing all that. He said,
"About Nancy—" and kept on looking toward the door of the
room they waited in.

"Men marry for money," Heimrich remarked, saying the
obvious. "Kill for it, too. Adams suspected, I suppose. Was
afraid—for Mrs. Blaine. Put a lock on the poison cupboard.
Found Compton breaking in and got killed for his—vigilance."

"You say nicotine." Olds was still looking at the door through
which word would come. "In her drink?"

Heimrich showed surprise, because he felt surprise.

"No—not in her drink. Mixed with the antiseptic," he said.
"Put on her cut fingers, for absorption through the skin. Absorbs
readily, nicotine does—through broken skin, especially. And
it's deadly stuff. So if you file a nasty sawtooth edge on a chair
arm, where somebody is sure to cut herself sooner or later, and
have a mixture of merthiolate and nicotine waiting—Nicotine

doesn't smell of tobacco until it's been exposed to air, you know. Well—"

A nurse came. She came smiling,

"She'll be all right," the nurse said. "One of you can go in now for a few minutes."

It was Heimrich's job to go, naturally. But there was not that much hurry. Martin Olds looked at Heimrich and his eyes asked a question—asked it anxiously. Heimrich answered with a nod, and Martin Olds went fast.

A catalytic agent, Heimrich thought, of Martin Olds, and walked out of the waiting room. An element which precipitates action. Specifically, a young man to whom pretty Nancy Blaine had turned once and might, now that he had reappeared, conceivably turn again. And if she had drifted to Olds, her money would drift with her. Compton couldn't chance that, of course.

But how had Charles Compton first betrayed himself to the wise old caretaker? How had Compton revealed what kind of man he was?

They would never know that. But the old man had won in the end—won through losing his own life. And, of course, through a good gardener's generosity with ground bone, which gives long, slow sustenance to questing roots.

THE SCENT OF MURDER

THE SCENT OF MURDER

Ronnie Beede had been free for forty-eight hours and he had a gun and he was a killer. Throughout Westchester and Putnam counties people locked their doors against Ronnie Beede.

He had escaped from the psychiatric ward of an upstate hospital and since then he had murdered twice. First he had killed a salesman who had picked him up on the road and after that a girl of sixteen who had been baby-sitting in a house he had broken into for food and clothes. The police were sure of the first: his fingerprints had been found on the salesman's car, which Beede had abandoned when it ran out of gas. They were not so sure about the girl. But her killing had been needless, wanton, and that looked like Ronnie Beede.

They knew a good deal about Beede—almost everything, except where he was. A big blond man in his middle twenties; a good-looking man with a friendly face and a wide, agreeable smile, and a slow, rather diffident way of speaking. The sort of attractive young man anyone might have picked up, even a person who should have known better. Probably the salesman had been bored and lonely when he stopped for Ronnie on a road above Peekskill. Ronnie had slugged him, then strangled him and thrown his body by the roadside. That was needless, too, but it was Ronnie's way. The gun he had now had been in the glove compartment of the salesman's car.

The girl had been killed in Mt. Kisco, and geography as well as wantonness made the police think of Ronnie Beede. If he was working his way home—killing his way home—Mt. Kisco would be on his route—on the route to a small, unpainted farmhouse on a back road between Brewster and Pawling. His mother waited there—a frail woman with a drawn face who

had trembled uncontrollably when Captain M. L. Heimrich
of the New York State Police spoke to her, although Heimrich
spoke gently, believing that Ronnie was no fault of hers. She
thought the fault the army's. "He was always a good boy until
he went into the army. The best son a mother ever—" She had
been unable to finish.

There was no telling whose fault Ronnie was, but that was
not Heimrich's problem—except that, as well as a policeman,
he was a man, and mankind worried him. It was easy enough
to put a word to Ronnie. He was a paranoic, knowing the
world was against him and killing to defend himself against
the world. *Mad Killer Strides Again*—that was the way a New
York City tabloid had headlined it that July morning, after the
girl's body had been found. The fault? It was not for the police
to decide. Their problem was to catch Beede—before he killed
again.

The news came on the car radio at four thirty-one in the
afternoon. The car, with Sergeant Charles Forniss driving, was
two miles east of Katonah on NY-22, heading west toward the
barracks at Hawthorne. Forniss set the siren going and the car
leaped—leaped through Katonah, with other cars flinching to
the curbs; screamed its way north and west for three miles and
a little more, and onto a side road and then, almost at once, up
a winding driveway between trees.

Forniss knew the way. Franklins were well-known the there-
abouts—Arthur Franklin was on the town planning board and
the library committee, and Martha Franklin had been active in
the garden club, although less lately than in the recent past.
It was hard to believe that a thing like this could happen to
people like the Franklins.

Their house was isolated, deep in ancient trees. It was probably the isolation and quiet that had brought murder there.

Heimrich and Forniss were the first of the police to arrive.
The front door of the house stood open; the screen which had
shielded it had been gashed near the knob. In the square hall

beyond the door, Arthur Franklin was sitting on a bench—sitting with his wrists resting on his knees and his hands dangling between them. He sat staring at the floor, which was in deep shadow. When Heimrich and Forniss crossed the porch, he got up slowly, heavily, then came to the door and looked at them with almost blank eyes.

"He killed her," Arthur Franklin said. He spoke, Heimrich thought, as if for sometime he had been saying the same words over and over in his mind. "For no reason at all. Anything he wanted—" Franklin did not finish; he pressed the palm of his right hand against his forehead and moved it slowly up his forehead. The hand ground dirt into the skin. He was a handsome man—heavy and in his late forties, but still handsome. He wore stained walking shorts and a blue shirt; he had been kneeling in earth and his knees were grimed with it. "For no reason at all," he repeated, and stepped back so that they could enter the hall.

Martha Franklin lay on the floor, on her back, in blood. She had been a tall woman and looked older by some years than her husband. The dead face was bony—even in death, austere and dominating. Up to now, Heimrich thought, looking down at her, she probably had always got her way. She must, Heimrich found himself thinking, have died in furious surprise that she—*she*—could thus be flouted. She had been shot through the head, from close in. She had fallen with her head toward a marble fireplace.

"I was down in the garden," Franklin said, without being asked. "If only I had been here—"He shook his head, then looked hard at Heimrich. "How many more are you going to let him kill?"

"Him?" Heimrich said.

"This—maniac," Franklin said. "The one in the newspapers. On the radio. What's his name?"

"Beede," Heimrich said. "Ronnie Beede."

"We'd have given him whatever he wanted," Franklin said. "Food, money—anything he wanted. To kill somebody for—for *nothing*." He looked down at the body of his wife, stunned, moving his head slowly from side to side.

There was no use staying in the hall where death was so visible. There was nothing immediately to be done there, and the others were on their way. Through the open door they could hear sirens, not far off. Gently, Heimrich guided the heavy man from the hall into a living room. "You were in the garden?" Heimrich said. "You didn't see anyone?"

"I heard somebody running," Franklin said. "And a shot. I didn't pay any attention to the shot. You hear them in the country, and it sounded a long way off. But then—somebody running off through the field. From the house." He stopped and stood shaking his head, as if in disbelief. "I was staking up the tomatoes," he said. He repeated it—"staking up the tomatoes"—as if this incongruity was monstrous.

"The garden," Heimrich said. "It's some distance from the house, I take it?"

"Over the hill," Franklin said. "Only place there's enough sun. If—if I'd only been here with her. I—" He shook his head quickly, this time as if to shake shadows out of his mind. "She was resting, probably," he went on. "Heard him break in—you saw the screen?"

"Yes," Heimrich said.

"Went to see what it was," Franklin said. "She would have. She was like that. And he shot her. Just like that. For no reason at all. For no—"

"Now, Mr. Franklin," Heimrich said. "The man you heard running. He ran past the garden?"

"Through the next field," Franklin said. "I was kneeling down among the vines. Had my back to the field. By the time I looked around he was gone. It was this man Beede, wasn't it?"

Heimrich said he supposed so. It had been done Ronnie Beede's way—wantonly, for no reason. "We're doing all—"

he began, and stopped, because Arthur Franklin was swaying on his feet. Heimrich moved quickly and caught Franklin around the shoulders. For an instant the man was dead weight in his grasp. Heimrich helped him to a chair, lowered him into it, holding the heavy man's wrists as he let him down, being pulled forward by Franklin's weight. Heimrich's nostrils were pinched.

"All right," Franklin said, after a moment. "It's nothing. Dizzy. Too much sun, maybe. Too much—everything."

"Naturally," Heimrich soothed. He heard a car door slam outside, heard feet on the porch. And then brakes squealed, and another car door opened and closed. The others were showing up. "Just sit and rest a minute, Mr. Franklin," Heimrich said, and went back to the hall.

They were getting cameras out. That came first. "Beede?" Forniss said, and Heimrich said, "Looks like it, doesn't it, Charlie? Mrs. Franklin surprised him and he killed her. And ran. Down past Mr. Franklin's garden. I'll go and have a look."

He went along a path, in the shade first, over a rise and down again, and then into the sun—the full sun a garden needs. It was a fine neat garden. Some day, Heimrich thought, he would like to have a garden like it—with bush limas ripening in long rows and tomato vines tied carefully to stakes. To his right, as he faced the garden, there was a stone fence, and beyond it a field of tall grass and blueberry bushes.

Heimrich went into Mr. Franklin's vegetable garden and squatted among the tomatoes. Franklin kept the vines trained to three stems by pinching off unwanted shoots. The stubs of many such were on the ground, withering in the sun. Franklin had missed some and Heimrich snipped two or three between thumb and forefinger. He smelled his fingers, nodded, and walked back to the house. He went through the now crowded hall and into the living room. Franklin sat where Heimrich had left him.

Heimrich went up to the seated man, lifted Franklin's right hand, and looked at it, while Franklin stared at him, then began to pull his hand away. The hand was grimed. Heimrich bent down and smelled it.

"What the hell?" Franklin said, and his voice was no longer dull—it was sharp, alert.

"Now, Mr. Franklin," Heimrich said. "You say you were working with the tomato plants?"

"I told you—" Franklin began, then stopped.

"Smell your hands yourself," Heimrich said. "Go on, Mr. Franklin."

But Franklin did not smell his hands. He began to stand up.

"No," Heimrich said, and Franklin sank back.

"Then," Heimrich said, "smell my fingers, Mr. Franklin," and held thumb and forefinger in front of Franklin's nose. "Very pungent odor tomato vines have, haven't they?" Heimrich said. "Quite unmistakable. When you handle them, the odor gets on your hands and stays. Until you wash the sap off, and then the water you wash in turns green. You know that, naturally. But—*it's not on your hands now, is it?* I noticed that when you were dizzy and I was helping you. No tomato smell. But— you hadn't washed your hands, had you? You dirtied them, yes—and your knees too—to show you'd just come from the garden. Took advantage of the fact there was a killer on the loose and—*why did you kill her, Mr. Franklin?* Merely because she was hard to live with? Or did she have the money?"

Franklin did not answer. But something happened to his eyes.

That sort of thing occurs now and then—a flaw in a lie is exposed and the lie falls, and the liar with it. Franklin had been careless, Heimrich pointed out to Sergeant Forniss somewhat later. If he had said he was in the garden hoeing beans he might easily have got away with it.

They trapped Ronnie Beede that evening. The trap was his mother's house and they let him walk into it. He was on his knees, with his face buried in his mother's lap, when they took him. He was shaking so hard that the frail woman shook with him.

SOURCES

Mr. and Mrs. North story.

"Pattern f or M urder," *T his Week* November 6 1 955. *E llery Queen's Mystery Magazine.* October, 1957

Captain M. L. Heimrich stories.

"Nobody Can Ask That," *This Week* April 8 1956. *Ellery Queen's Mystery Magazine.* May, 1957

"The Searching Cats," *This Week* December 2 1956. *Ellery Queen's Mystery Magazine.* February, 1958

"Dead Boys Don't Remember," *Ellery Queen's Mystery Magazine.* July, 1958

"All Men Make Mistakes," *This Week* May 12 1957. *Ellery Queen's Mystery Magazine.* November, 1958

"Hit-and-Run," *This Week* April 14 1957. *Ellery Queen's Mystery Magazine.* July, 1959

"Captain Heimrich Stumbles," *Ellery Queen's Mystery Magazine.* November, 1959

"If They Give Him Time," *This Week* October 27 1957. *Ellery Queen's Mystery Magazine.* February, 1960

"Cat of Dreams," *This Week* December 7 1958. *Ellery Queen's Mystery Magazine.* May, 1960

"A Winter's Tale," *Ellery Queen's Mystery Magazine.* February, 1961

"The Accusing Smoke," *This Week* April 19 1959. *Ellery Queen's Mystery Magazine.* August, 1961

"Flair for Murder," *Ellery Queen's Mystery Magazine.* October, 1965

"The Scent of Murder," *Ellery Queen's Mystery Magazine.* August, 1960

Flair for Murder

Flair for Murder is printed on 60-pound paper, and is designed by Satheesh Embar. The type is Book Antiqua, a style that imitates Renaissance caligraphy. The cover is by Jackie Webber. The first edition was published in two forms: trade softcover, perfect bound; and one hundred copies sewn in cloth. *Flair for Murder* was printed by Southern Ohio Printers and bound by Cincinnati Bindery. The book was published in March 2024 by Crippen & Landru Publishers, Inc., Cincinnati, OH.

Crippen & Landru, Publishers

P. O. Box 532057

Cincinnati, OH 45253

Web: www.crippenlandru.com

E-mail: info@crippenlandru.com

Crippen & Landru publishes first editions of short-story collections by important detective and mystery writers.

This is the best edited, most attractively packaged line of mystery books introduced in this decade. The books are equally valuable to collectors and readers. — *Mystery Scene Magazine*

The specialty publisher with the most star-studded list is Crippen & Landru, which has produced short story collections by some of the biggest names in contemporary crime fiction. — *Ellery Queen's Mystery Magazine*

God Bless Crippen & Landru. — *The Strand Magazine*

A monument in the making is appearing year by year from Crippen & Landru, a small press devoted exclusively to publishing the criminous short story. — *Alfred Hitchcock's Mystery Magazine*

CRIPPEN & LANDRU LOST CLASSICS

Crippen & Landru is proud to publish a series of new short-story collections by great authors of the past who specialized in traditional mysteries. Each book collects stories from crumbling pages of old newspapers, and pulp, digest, and slick magazines, and most of the stories have been "lost" since their first publication.

We have been frequently asked for a complete list of "Lost Classics." Prices are given for titles currently in print; other books are unavailable from the publisher.

Murder, Mystery and Malone by Craig Rice, edited by Jeffrey A. Marks. 2002. eBook $8.99

The Avenging Chance and Other Mysteries from Roger Sheringham's Casebook by Anthony Berkeley, edited by Tony Medawar and Arthur Robinson. 2004. Second edition enlarged, 2015. Trade softcover, $19.00. eBook $8.99

Banner Deadlines: The Impossible Files of Senator Brooks U. Banner by Joseph Commings, edited by Robert Adey; memoir by Edward D. Hoch. 2004. eBook $8.99

The Danger Zone and Other Stories by Erie Stanley Gardner, edited by Bill Pronzini. 2004. eBook $8.99

Who Was Guilty? Two Dime Novels by Philip S. Wame/ Howard W. Macy, edited by Marlena E. Bremseth. 2005. Cloth, $29.00.

Slot-Machine Kelly by Dennis Lynds writing as Michael Collins, introduction by Robert J. Randisi. 2005. Trade softcover, $19.00.

The Casebook of Sidney Zoom by Erie Stanley Gardner, edited by Bill Pronzini. 2006. eBook $8.99

The Exploits of the Patent Leather Kid by Erie Stanley Gardner, edited by Bill Pronzini. 2010. eBook $8.99

The Extraordinary Cases of Barnabas Hildreth by Vincent Cornier, edited by Mike Ashley. 2011. eBook $8.99

The Casebook of Jonas P. Jonas and Other Mysteries by Elizabeth Ferrars, edited by John Cooper. 2012. eBook $8.99

Night Call and Other Stories of Suspense by Charlotte Armstrong, edited by Rick Cypert and Kirby McCauley. 2014. eBook $8.99

Sequel to Murder by Anthony Gilbert, edited by John Cooper. Full cloth in dust jacket, $29.00. Trade softcover, $19.00.

Hildegarde Withers: Final Riddles? by Stuart Palmer with an introduction by Steven Saylor. Full cloth in dust jacket, $29.00. Trade softcover, $19.00

Shooting Script by William Link and Richard Levinson, edited by Joseph Goodrich. Full cloth in dust jacket, signed and numbered by the families, $47.00. Trade softcover, $22.00.

The Man Who Solved Mysteries by William Brittain with an introduction by Josh Pachter. Full cloth in dust jacket, $29.00. Trade softcover, $19.00

Constant Hearses and Other Revolutionary Mysteries by Edward D. Hoch. Full cloth in dust jacket, signed and numbered by Brian Skupin, $45.00. Trade softcover, $19.00.

SUBSCRIPTIONS

Crippen & Landru offers discounts to individuals and institutions who place Subscriptions for its forthcoming publications, either the Regular Series or the Lost Classics or (preferably) both. Collectors can thereby guarantee receiving limited editions, and readers won't miss any favorite stories. Subscribers receive a specially commissioned story as a gift at the end of the year. Please write or e-mail: orders@crippenlandru.com for more details.

Milton Keynes UK
Ingram Content Group UK Ltd.
UKHW010704260424
441811UK00001B/132